Bert tried to rescue the treasure box.

The Bobbsey Twins Solve a Mystery

The Bobbsey Twins
Solve a Mystery

By
LAURA LEE HOPE

GROSSET & DUNLAP
Publishers   *New York*

THE BOBBSEY TWINS SOLVE A MYSTERY

PRINTED IN THE UNITED STATES OF AMERICA

ISBN: 0-448-08027-3

CONTENTS

CONTENTS

CHAPTER I

THE CAPTAIN'S SECRET

THE Bobbsey Twins were finally settled in But-tonball Cottage at Storm Haven, the seashore place where they were to spend the summer. One of the first things Freddie Bobbsey did when he got there was to buy a small toy sailboat.

"Where did you get it, Freddie?" asked Bert, who was admiring the trim little craft his small brother was hurrying to sail on the lagoon behind the Edgemere Hotel.

"Bought it in a store on Main Street," Freddie answered, as he straightened the mast of his little sailing vessel.

"They have a lot of boats bigger than this one," said Flossie, who was so much interested in what she and Freddie were going to do that she was carrying her doll upside down. "They have some with two sails."

"Then why didn't you get a larger boat, Freddie?" asked Nan Bobbsey, shaking her dark hair back out of her eyes. The wind that was blowing it was not good for neatly combed hair, but it was good for sailing boats.

"I didn't have enough money to get a bigger one," answered the small Bobbsey boy. "I had only enough for this one. But it's pretty good, isn't it, Bert?"

"Yes, it looks like a regular craft," said Bert, taking it from his brother and examining it closely. "It has a keel and a rudder that can be set."

"Say, you know a lot about boats, don't you, Bert?" asked Flossie.

"Not as much as I'd like to," Bert answered. "Now that we're going to stay all summer at this seashore place, maybe I can learn more, though."

"I'd like to know how to sail a real boat that we can ride in," spoke Nan.

"Girls don't sail boats—only men do," declared Freddie.

"Yes, they do," broke in Flossie. "Don't you remember when we were down near the village dock before you bought yours, Freddie, that we saw a lady pulling up the sail on a pussy boat?"

"Pussy boat!" exclaimed Nan, laughing.

"I guess she means a cat boat," explained Bert. "A cat boat is a small boat with only one mast."

"Mine's a cat boat, then," went on Freddie. "It has one mast."

"It takes more than a mast to make a cat boat," Bert declared. "It's big enough for people to get in and a captain steers it. The sail can be hauled up and let down, too. You can't lower the sail of your boat, Freddie."

"I don't want to take down my sail," spoke Freddie. "I'm going to leave it up. The wind is blowing so hard now that Flossie and I are going to that lake back of the hotel and sail my boat."

"Don't fall in," warned Bert. He and Nan, after having helped Mrs. Bobbsey and Dinah, the jolly colored cook, to straighten up the cottage, had started downtown to buy a few things their mother wanted. Before they had gone very far they met Flossie and Freddie.

"I won't fall in," Freddie promised.

"Anyhow, if he does, it won't hurt him," added Flossie. "The lake isn't deep."

"It's plenty deep at the end down near the

hotel," Bert said. "They have swimming and diving contests there at the close of the summer season."

"Do they?" asked Nan. "That must be nice. Oh, I think it's just lovely here at Storm Haven," she went on, looking out across the blue water of the safe and sheltered bay in which many vessels were sailing, steaming, and riding at anchor. Storm Haven was a good name for this seashore summer resort. Many a boat had put in there so as to be protected from the storms that often came up on the big ocean which was on the other side. The bay was curved like the horns of a new moon, and there were several little villages all around the shore edges. Back of these lay hills, valleys, and stretches of woods and swamps where, it was said, various kinds of berries grew.

"Yes, Storm Haven is a fine place," said Bert. "I think it's the nicest summer resort we have ever visited."

"And we have been to a lot of nice ones," added Nan. "I'm glad there's such a big hotel nearby. Bert, perhaps you and I may go to one of the junior dances sometime."

"I don't care about dancing," Bert said.

"I mean just to watch them," Nan explained.

"Oh, well, maybe I'll take you over if you want to watch," Bert agreed. "But I'a rather see the swimming and diving contests."

"We'll see those, too," said Nan.

Flossie and Freddie were starting off toward the body of water behind the hotel. Some called it a lagoon, while others termed it a lake. It really was the latter, however, quite deep at the hotel end where there was a bathing pavilion.

"Bert," Nan said suddenly.

"What is it?" asked her brother.

"Do you think we had better let those two children go off by themselves to sail that boat on the lake?" asked Nan. "One of them might fall in."

"What do you want me to do?" asked Bert. "Take Freddie's boat away from him? He'll set up a big howl if I do."

"No, don't take it away," suggested Nan. "But let's you and I watch them for a little while. We have time. Then we'll know they'll be safe. We can do mother's shopping later."

"Well, all right," Bert agreed.

He did not make any fuss about it, as Nan feared he might do. To be frank, Bert was strangely interested in Freddie's toy boat. It had been some time since he had had a little sailboat of his own, and now that he was at a place where there was a chance to launch one he began to think he might get one for himself.

"But I want a bigger one than Freddie has," he decided. "I'll go watch how his sails, though." So he was content to go with Nan, whose sole purpose was to make sure that neither Flossie nor Freddie would fall into the lake.

Bert and Nan followed Flossie and Freddie down a path that led to the end of the lake farthest from the hotel. As the younger twins hurried on ahead of the other two, Bert said with a laugh:

"It surprises me that if Freddie went into a shop with money in his pocket, he didn't buy a toy fire engine. Remember what a fuss he made when we were coming away, Nan, because Mother forgot to pack his big engine that squirts water from a spring pump?"

"I should say I do!" laughed Nan. "Yes, it is strange that Freddie didn't buy a little fire engine instead of a toy boat."

During most of his few years, Freddie Bobbsey had said he was going to be a fireman when he grew up. He talked so much about it that his father nicknamed him his "little fireman," just as he had called Flossie his "little fat fairy."

Freddie, who was hurrying on ahead with his twin sister, overheard what Bert and Nan had just said about him. He turned and called:

"I could have bought a toy fire engine. They had one in the store, but it didn't squirt water so I didn't buy it. I got this boat instead. Anyhow, maybe I won't be a fireman any more."

"What are you going to be?" asked Nan, looking at Bert and laughing a little.

"I'm going to be a sailor," Freddie decided. "Now that we're going to be at the seashore all summer, I might as well be a sailor."

"And I'm going to be one, too," added Flossie. "We saw a lady at the dock, and she was on a sailboat."

"And she had pants on," said Freddie.

"Pants—on a lady!" exclaimed Nan.

"Oh, a lot of the girls and ladies down here dress just like boys," said Bert. "I guess it's easier for a lady to be a sailor in pants than it is in skirts. Skirts get in the way."

"Yes, they do, if they're too long," agreed Nan. "But I'd like to see this lady who dresses like a sailor."

"I'll show her to you after I sail my boat if she hasn't gone away," promised Freddie.

In a short while the four twins were standing on the edge of the little lake. The hotel was some distance away. Around the end of the lagoon several summer vacationists were swimming, diving, or otherwise having a good time in or near the water. The hotel faced the beach, and on the sands there were more swimmers and several boys and girls out in canoes, rowboats and sailboats. The bay of Storm Haven was not rough like the ocean outside, and small boats could be sailed safely. Farther out there were larger craft. Bert had been admiring one of them. It was a big, three-masted schooner, though all the sails were furled and the vessel lay at anchor.

"That's the kind of a ship I'd like to sail," said Bert admiringly, as Freddie put his small toy down on the water.

"You'll have to grow up before you can sail a big boat like that," spoke Flossie.

"Well, we are growing up," declared Nan. "I heard Mother and Father talking about it the other day. They said you and I were growing up fast. And we're older than when we were at the seashore last time, Bert."

"Yes, I guess we are," he agreed. "So are Flossie and Freddie."

A little breeze was blowing across the lake, spreading out the sail on Freddie's toy boat and heading it across to the other side.

"Look at my boat go!" cried Freddie, dancing up and down in delight.

"Yes, it sails pretty well," admitted Bert.

"But look!" cried Flossie. "It's going way off— to the other side of the lake. Oh, Freddie, you'll never get it back again!"

Freddie looked at Bert. The little boy had not counted on this.

"Why didn't you set the rudder so your boat would go around in a sort of curve and come back to you?" asked Bert. "You should have done that."

"Aye, that he should, my lad!" exclaimed a deep, hearty, but friendly voice behind the Bobbsey twins. "And another thing, the little sailor should have a boat with a jib sail on her. Then it would be easier to have it come back to him."

The children turned to see a tall man standing near the edge of the lake. His face was much more tanned than those of other summer visitors at Storm Haven. He looked like a sailor. However, to make sure of it, Bert asked:

"Do you know all about sailing toy boats, sir?"

"Not only toy boats, my lad, but real boats,

also," was the answer. "That's my craft anchored out there." He pointed a brown, stubby finger at the three-masted schooner in the bay. "That's the *Debby D*", he said.

"What does that mean?" asked Flossie, who stepped out from behind Nan where she had been hidden, for the moment, from the gaze of the sailor. "What does *Debby D* mean?"

"Why! Why, what a picture you are, my child!" exclaimed the old sailor. He seemed strangely excited at seeing Flossie with her blue eyes and golden hair. "What a lovely little girl!" murmured the sailor. "I wish—I wonder. No, it can't be possible," he went on in a low voice.

He acted so queer and spoke so strangely, that Bert and Nan looked at each other in wonderment. Then, almost as quickly as the peculiar mood had come over the sailor, it passed away.

"There, there!" he murmured. "I shouldn't trouble children like you with my secret. Let it pass. Forget about it. Sail your boat."

"It's sailing, all right," Freddie exclaimed, "but I want it to come back to me. I'm afraid I'll lose it."

"No, you won't lose it, my little man," said the sailor captain, "for you can walk around to the other side of this lagoon and get it when it goes ashore. There isn't enough wind to pile her up a wreck on the rocks, as I once did."

"Were you shipwrecked, sir?" asked Bert.

"Yes, my lad, and on a lonely desert island, too. Regular Robinson Crusoe I was, for fair, shipwrecked, and all by myself. But that was long ago."

He continued to gaze at Flossie, but she and Freddie were more interested in their toy boat than they were in the sailor.

"I'd like to hear about the shipwreck," said Bert.

Though Nan did not say so, she wanted to hear about the secret. As for Flossie and Freddie, all they cared about was the toy boat which was now bobbing along under a stiff breeze way over at the other side of the lake.

"Well, maybe I'll tell you some day," promised the sailor captain. "I'm on shore leave for a while. But I'll soon be hoisting my anchor again. Now about this toy boat: she isn't rigged right. What do those toy store folks know about rigging a boat? Nothing, if you ask me!"

"What does she need?" asked Bert eagerly.

"She needs a jib sail, for one thing. And I think her rudder is wrongly rigged. By the way," he went on, "are you children going to be here for a day or two?"

"We'll be here all summer," said Nan. "We're staying at Buttonball Cottage." It was so named because there were so many buttonball, or syca- more, trees about it. Sycamore trees are the best for growing near the ocean, for the salt air does not make them wither and die as it does maples or other trees.

"Well, if you're going to be here for the sum- mer I'll see you again," said the sailor. "How would it be if you were to meet me here after din- ner? I'll come down and show you how to rig this boat properly. I'll make a jib for her and then, my little man," he said to Freddie, "when you start her out from harbor I'll show you how to set the rudder to bring her back almost to the place from which she sailed."

"That would be great!" said Bert.

"Dandy!" cried Freddie, starting on the run with Flossie to get the boat, which was now near- ing the other side of the lake.

"We'll meet you here, then," said Nan.

"Aye, aye, my lass!" murmured the sailor. But he did not look at Nan. His eyes followed the blue- eyed and golden-haired Flossie.

"I wonder what his secret is?" said Bert, as the sailor walked off toward the beach.

"I'd like to know myself," murmured Nan.

"Let's ask him this afternoon," exclaimed Bert.

"That's a good idea," agreed Nan.

CHAPTER II

ON THE SCHOONER

BERT and Nan Bobbsey followed their brother and sister around the edge of the lake toward the place where the toy ship was moving ashore. As they neared the hotel they saw one of the elevator boys coming out. Bert and Nan had met him the first night of their arrival at Storm Haven, when the Bobbsey family had gone to dinner at the hotel.

This elevator boy, whose name was Harry Sunderland, had given Flossie and Freddie drinks from the ice-water cooler in the lobby. Therefore, the children recognized him at once. He now smiled and waved.

"Where are you going?" asked Harry.

"My brother's toy boat blew over to the other side," Bert explained. "We're going to see that he gets it back."

"Oh, yes," Harry remarked, looking in the direction toward which Bert pointed. "This lagoon is quite a place for sailing toy boats. Later in the season the hotel will hold a real regatta here for them."

"You mean for little fellows like Freddie?" asked Bert.

"Yes, and for bigger fellows and bigger boats, too," said Harry. "Some boys older than I am enter their craft and win prizes. I shouldn't be allowed to do so, as I work for the hotel, but you might enter a big toy boat if you had one," he added.

"Really?"

"Sure! Why, some of them are this long," and Harry held his hands about two feet apart.

"Those are some boats!" exclaimed Bert, admiringly.

"They sure are. Besides holding a toy boat regatta, the hotel has races for small cat boats which are sailed by one or two people. They give silver cups for prizes in that group. There is one class for boys of seventeen and eighteen years. They take out a passenger. Then there are cat boat races for boys about twelve."

"That's nearer my age," said Bert with a smile.

"But do they enter such boats on this little lake?" asked Nan.

"No, those races are held out in the bay, where

you see that three-master," Harry explained, pointing to the craft that had been indicated by the sailor who had such a mysterious secret. "But the toy boat races take place on the hotel lake."

"We just met the captain of that schooner," went on Bert, looking out toward the *Debby D*. "He's going to show my little brother how to rig his toy boat better."

"Well, Captain Van Pelt ought to know how," said Harry.

"Is that his name?" asked Nan.

"Yes, Captain Amzi Van Pelt," went on the elevator boy. "He's stopping at our hotel temporarily. Something went wrong with his schooner after he sailed back here, so he put in for repairs. He told me he was making a search of some kind, so he thought he'd live ashore for about a week. That's how he happens to be at our hotel. He's a nice, kind man, and never makes any fuss if the elevator isn't there the minute he wants it."

"What's he searching for ashore?" asked Bert, highly interested.

"I don't know exactly," Harry answered. "He's sort of odd. I guess he has a secret he isn't telling anybody."

"He spoke to us about a secret," Nan said, "but

he didn't say what it was. He looked at my little sister as if he wanted to talk to her about something."

"Yes, he's very fond of children, is Captain Van Pelt," admitted Harry. "I've noticed him as he sits in the hotel lobby. If any guests come in with a little girl he can hardly take his eyes off her. Maybe his secret has to do with someone like that."

"Perhaps," agreed Bert. "But say, Harry," he went on, "I'd like to hear more about this boat regatta."

"Thinking of entering?"

"I'd like to."

"In the big toy boat class?"

"Yes, in that one and the small cat boat class."

"Daddy would never let you sail a real boat, Bert!" exclaimed Nan.

"He might," said Bert. "He did once when he was with me, but not very far. I'd like to learn how to sail a real boat."

"Well, down here at Storm Haven is a good place in which to learn," said Harry with a laugh.

He had to be on his way, so Bert and Nan continued on toward the other side of the lake, whither Flossie and Freddie were hastening. Bert was thinking about his chances of getting a real sail-boat. Nan was wondering what secret Captain Van Pelt could have that had to do with a little girl like Flossie.

As Bert and Nan were approaching their small brother and sister, they saw Freddie reach over to pick up his boat, which had now touched shore. A sudden puff of wind carried the toy craft out a little ways, and in trying to grasp it Freddie lost his balance and went splash into the lake.

"Oh, look!" screamed Nan.

"He'll get out all right—the water isn't over his ankles," said Bert. Even as he spoke Freddie scrambled to his feet.

"But he's soaking wet! We'll have to hurry home with him!" said Nan, starting to run to the place where Freddie was standing in stunned surprise, the water dripping from his clothes. Flossie did not seem to know whether to laugh or to cry.

Now, for just a moment I want to tell my new readers something about the Bobbsey Twins, and let them get an idea as to what the four of them did in the other books of this series. The first volume was called "The Bobbsey Twins." It told how Bert and Nan, the older twins, and Flossie and Freddie, the younger ones, lived with their father and mother in Lakeport. With them stayed fat, black, jolly Dinah, the cook, and her husband, Sam Johnson, who worked about the house and garden. Mr Bobbsey was in the lumber business.

The Bobbsey twins had many good times together, all of which are related in the various books. They had been to the country, seashore and mountains many times on summer vacations, and had gone camping and treasure-hunting, too.

In the book just before the one you are now reading, called "The Bobbsey Twins On An Airplane Trip," the four children had some strange and entertaining adventures. Summer had come again, and the twins were at the seashore. It looked very much as if they were on the trail of a mystery. "For," thought Nan to herself as she hurried to look after poor, drenched Freddie, "the secret of Captain Van Pelt might easily be a mystery. It would be such fun to solve it!"

As Bert had said, Freddie was in no danger, but he was quite wet, and looked very pitiful with his clothes drenched and his hair as straight as a string.

"You must come home at once!" decided Nan.

"But I want to get my boat!" protested Freddie. The little craft was on the lake, way beyond him.

"I'll get it for you," offered Bert. "You and Flossie go home with Nan."

"Not without my boat!" said Freddie firmly.

"But you're all wet!" cried Nan, "and if you stand around with wet clothes on you'll take cold."

"Pooh, it's too warm to take cold," objected Freddie. "Get my boat, Bert, and then I'll go home."

Bert tried to reach out for the bobbing toy boat, but his arms were not quite long enough.

"Look out, or you'll fall in yourself!" Nan warned him.

"Here! Let me help!" said a voice, and the children looked around to see one of the men employed at the hotel to keep the grounds neat and the grass cut. He had a rake with him, and with this he easily reached out and hauled Freddie's boat ashore.

"Thank you," said Bert, taking it from the water. "Now we'll all go home. Gosh, but you are a sight, Freddie!"

There was considerable excitement in Buttonball Cottage when the twins finally arrived.

"Mercy! What happened to you, Freddie?" asked his mother.

"Oh, yo' po' honey lamb!" murmured Dinah.

"Come wif me an' I'll git yo' all some dry clothes!"

"Was he in any peril?" asked Mrs. Bobbsey. "If he was, I must tell your father when he comes down this evening and he'll have to scold Freddie."

"He wasn't in any real danger," Bert said, explaining how the little accident had happened. "He just fell in at the edge."

At lunch time, with Freddie in dry clothes, the events of the morning were discussed, and Mrs. Bobbsey was told about Captain Van Pelt.

"He knows a lot about boats," Bert declared. "I wish he would teach me something."

"Maybe he will," said Mrs. Bobbsey with a smile. She and Dinah were to be busy that afternoon getting the cottage more completely to rights. Mr. Bobbsey, who had gone back to Lakeport after bringing his family to the shore, was to come down for a few nights during the first two weeks. After that he would stay up in the city and visit them while on his vacation.

True to his promise, Captain Van Pelt met the Bobbsey twins at the little lake during the middle of the afternoon. Freddie had his toy boat with him.

"Tell you what it is, my hearties!" exclaimed the

sailor, looking sharply at Flossie. "I'll need some tools and material for fixing this little chap's toy boat. I haven't them at the hotel where I'm boarding. I wonder if you could come out on my schooner—the *Debby D?*" He pointed to the three-master.

"You mean you'll take us aboard her and fix Freddie's boat there?" asked Bert, his eyes shining.

"Aye, aye, my lad, if your mother will let you. Do you want to inspect her?"

"I'll say we do!" cried Bert.

"But how can we get out to her?" asked Flossie.

"I have a rowboat down at the dock which I use for making trips to my schooner. If Pegleg Baldwin is ashore now he'll row you out, otherwise I will."

"Who's Pegleg Baldwin?" asked Bert.

"Oh, he's one of my sailors—has a wooden leg, but is good enough for all that. He's a jolly sort of chap, and tattooed like a Fiji Islander."

"Tattooed!" exclaimed Bert. "You mean he has letters and pictures printed on his skin in blue ink?"

"Pictures is no name for it!" chuckled Captain Van Pelt. "And not only in blue ink but red, too. You'll see."

"Is he the only sailor you have?" asked Freddie.

"Bless your main topsails, no!" laughed Captain Van Pelt. "I need several men on my schooner. But while she's been laid up for repairs, which are almost finished now, the crew has been on shore leave. I just keep Pegleg Baldwin for an anchor watch. Perhaps we'd better ask your mother if it's all right for you to go aboard."

"Come on!" urged Nan.

Walking beside Captain Van Pelt, the Bobbsey Twins were soon at Buttonball Cottage.

"Mother," Bert said, "this is Captain Van Pelt. And this is my mother, Mrs. Bobbsey, Captain."

"What!" cried the sailor, as he looked first at her, then at the twins. "You don't mean your name is Bobbsey?"

"Why, sure it is!" Freddie laughed. "We're the Bobbsey twins!"

"Mr. Richard Bobbsey, of Lakeport, ma'am?" he asked.

"That is my husband's name, Captain."

"Why, then we ought to be friends!" laughed the sailor. "I do business with Mr. Bobbsey," he added. "In fact, I delivered a schooner-load of lumber from Georgia to him two weeks ago. I haven't had a cargo since. My boat needed some repairs so I put in here to have 'em made as well as to do a little searching on my own account," he added. "That has nothing to do with lumber, though."

"It's a mysterious secret," Nan whispered to her mother. Mrs. Bobbsey did not pay much attention to what Nan said just then, as the Captain went on:

"And to think I should meet the Bobbsey twins here! It's great!"

"We are happy, too," agreed Mrs. Bobbsey. "I have often heard my husband speak of doing business with you."

"May we go out to his schooner?" asked Bert. "He's going to fix Freddie's boat."

"Won't they disturb you, Captain Van Pelt?" asked their mother.

"Not at all! I love children! I ought to have some of my own, if I could find 'em. But I won't go into that now. They'll be as welcome on the *Debby D* as the flowers in May. All aboard! Come along, my hearties!"

Eager and delighted, the Bobbsey twins accompanied Captain Van Pelt to the main wharf of Storm Haven. There the rowboat was tied up. On the dock stood a sailor with a wooden peg leg.

"Just in time, Peg!" said Captain Van Pelt to him. "Take me and these children out to the schooner."

"Aye, aye, sir," answered the sailor, as he led them down a gangway to the float, which went up and down with the tide. Nan and the others noticed that he had red and blue designs tattooed on his hands and wrists. How many there were on his body could only be guessed at.

"Bet there are a hundred," whispered Freddie.

After rowing a short while the group reached the sailing vessel. Bert and Nan climbed up the accommodation ladder that was over the side, and helped Flossie and Freddie to come after them. Captain Van Pelt followed, as did Pegleg Baldwin, but not until he had made the craft fast to the little platform of the accommodation ladder.

"Welcome to the *Debby D*, my dears," cried Captain Van Pelt. "And as soon as you have had time to take a look around, I'll get at fixing this young sailor's boat."

Highly interested, Bert, his sisters and brothers looked about the deck. No other sailors were to be seen. There were pieces of wood and chips about, as if some carpenters had recently been there.

"The repairs are about finished," said Captain

Van Pelt, as he kicked aside some of the wood shavings. "I'll soon be sailing away again."

Just then, from somewhere below, a voice shouted:

"Let me out! Let me out! Help! Help! He's got me by the throat! Let me out!"

CHAPTER III

OFF ON A VOYAGE

BERT and the other twins started, but to their surprise Captain Van Pelt paid not the slightest attention to the cries.

"Help! Help! Let me out!"

The owner of the *Debby D* had picked up a small piece of wood from among the shavings on the deck.

"This will do nicely for the jib boom of the new sail I am going to put on your boat, Freddie," said the Captain. "You brought it with you, I see."

"Yes, it's here," said Freddie. He had kept a tight hold on it all the way out from the dock to the schooner.

"But Captain," said Bert, as once again the cries for help came from below, "hadn't you better let that man out before you bother with Freddie's boat? He seems to be in trouble."

"Terrible trouble!" echoed Nan, her eyes wide open with wonderment.

Again a shout sounded.

"Help! Help! Let me out! If you don't let me out I'll sink the ship!"

"This big ship can't sink, can it, Captain?" asked Freddie.

"Anyhow, hadn't we better do something?" asked Bert. "If you want any help, Captain Van Pelt——"

The captain still seemed to pay no heed to the cries, but was calmly rummaging among some pieces of cloth. Bert looked at Pegleg Baldwin, who was thumping his way over the deck after having made fast the rowboat. The wooden-legged sailor was laughing.

"If you don't let me out I'll bite you!" yelled the voice from below. Finally Captain Van Pelt, apparently satisfied that what he had picked up would do for a new rigging on Freddie's boat, said:

"Oh, there goes Mr. Green again."

"Aye, aye, sir," answered Pegleg. "He's been yelling his head off ever since we came aboard, but you've been so busy thinking of this little lad's boat, Captain, that you didn't pay any attention to him."

"Yes, Mr. Green is making a bit of a noise," agreed the commander of the *Debby D.*

"Let me out! Let me out!"

"Aren't you going to let him out?" asked Nan rather timidly.

"If you don't he'll bite," added Freddie.

"He may bite anyway," chuckled the captain. "I expect he wants to bite into a cracker. Bring him up, Pegleg," he went on. "The children may like to see him."

Wondering who Mr. Green might be, and what he had done that he should be imprisoned below deck, the Bobbsey twins waited.

Up the companionway stairs came thumping Pegleg Baldwin. As his head appeared above the deck, the children saw a large wire cage and in it a big parrot. Most of its feathers were bright green, with here and there a dash of red and yellow.

"Ha! Ha! Ha!" shrieked the parrot. "I'm out! I'm out! I'm going to bite a cracker!"

"Yes, and if you bite anything else I'll send you below again!" said Captain Van Pelt with a laugh. "Put him in a shady place, Pegleg, get him a couple of crackers, and then look around and see how much more there is to be done on my schooner. All the workmen have gone ashore, I see. They must be nearly finished. I'll be calling my crew back and sailing again soon."

"Aye, aye, sir!" answered Pegleg, as he put the parrot's cage down in a shady spot and thrust some crackers through the wires.

"Now go stand on your head!" commanded the parrot as, with his black beak and blacker tongue, he began to bite the crackers.

"Is that Mr. Green?" asked Nan, laughing.

"That's right," said Captain Van Pelt. "He's a good talker, and you aren't the first ones he's fooled into thinking he's one of the sailors kept prisoner down below. Oh, he's clever, is Mr. Green."

The Bobbsey twins stood around the bird's cage for a while, watching him eat the crackers and listening to him talk. He could speak a number of sentences which sounded almost human.

Then, while Nan and Flossie were being escorted about the vessel by Pegleg, who offered to show them the cabins and other parts, Bert and Freddie watched Captain Van Pelt put the new jib sail on the little boy's boat.

"The jib, you see," explained the captain, "is a small triangular sail on the bow, or front of the boat. All your boat had when you bought it, Freddie, was the so-called mainsail. Without anyone on board to steer it according to the direction from which the wind blew, you could not very well send it out and have it come back to you.

"With the jib I am going to put on I think it will go better. Also, I intend to change the rudder so that it will steer differently."

"That'll be fine," said Freddie.

"If I should get a bigger toy boat," said Bert, "and it needs a different rigging to help me win a prize in the toy ship regatta at the hotel lagoon, would you show me how to change it, Captain Van Pelt?"

"Indeed I will, my lad," was the answer, "if I'm here at the time. I'll have to be sailing pretty soon, though, for I am making a search for someone. I don't know that I'll have any success, but I must keep on trying."

Bert fancied that Captain Van Pelt looked sad. He thought it might have something to do with the secret mystery at which the sailor had hinted.

"I'll be back here again," went on the captain. "And if I can help you, I certainly will. Now to fix Freddie's boat."

This did not take long. A small, triangular bit of cloth was fastened to the top of the mast of the toy ship. One end of the jib sail was also fastened to the "bowsprit," which is that long, slender stick of wood thrust out from a ship's bow. On the lower edge of the new sail the captain fastened a small piece of wood.

"This," he explained, "is the jib-boom. Not all jib sails have a boom, but all mainsails do. Anyhow, we'll put one on your ship."

"Say, it looks a lot bigger!" exclaimed Freddie, when the toy ship was handed back to him. "I'd like to try it on the lagoon."

"Well, you'll have to go ashore up near the hotel to do that," said the captain. "I'll be going back presently and will take all of you with me. But don't you two boys want to look around my ship?"

You may be sure Bert and Freddie did. They joined Nan and Flossie, who were with Pegleg, while Captain Van Pelt went to his cabin to look over some of his ship's books and papers.

"I'd like to take a sail on this schooner," said Bert.

Perhaps Flossie and Freddie also wished to do this, but they said nothing about it, for they were busy listening to Mr. Green. The parrot was saying many funny things after his lunch of crackers.

Toward the close of the afternoon Captain Van Pelt ordered Pegleg to get the rowboat ready, and they all got into it for the trip back to the dock.

"If all goes well," said the captain, "I'll take you children for a short sail on the *Debby D* before I go away on my next trip."

"That will be great!" said Bert.

"Wonderful!" agreed Nan.

In a short time the children were again on shore. Captain Van Pelt, after telling Pegleg Baldwin to go back to the craft and remain there all night as a guard, went up to the hotel. Nan and Flossie hurried to Buttonball Cottage, while Bert and Freddie went to the lagoon to try out the little ship.

The tiny craft went much better. When the rudder was adjusted, as Captain Van Pelt had suggested, the toy sailed out in a large circle, then came back to the boys at almost the very place from which it had started.

When Mr. Bobbsey came to the cottage that evening, he was glad to learn that his friend, Captain Van Pelt, had been so kind to the children.

"He said he'd take us for a sail on his schooner," remarked Nan.

"Do you think it will be safe, Dick?" asked Mrs. Bobbsey of her husband.

"Oh, yes, we need have no fear for the children when they are with Captain Van Pelt. I hardly think I'll get a chance to see him this trip, as I must take an early morning train back to Lakeport. But as he says he is coming back to Storm Haven soon, I'll get a chance to talk to him before the summer is over."

"Is he going to bring you more lumber?" asked Bert.

"He may."

"Do you know why he seems so sad?" asked Nan, "and what his secret mystery is?"

"No, Nan, I don't," answered her father. "But sometimes sailors are strange men. Being virtually alone on the ocean so much of the time makes them different, I suppose. If the captain takes you sailing, he may explain his mystery to you."

"I hope he does," said Nan.

Mr. Bobbsey went back to his lumber yard the next morning. Nan helped her mother and Dinah about the cottage while Flossie found a little girl, living nearby, with whom to play. Bert and Freddie went to sail the plaything again.

"Yes," remarked Bert, when he saw how well Freddie's newly-rigged craft behaved, "I'm going to save up and buy a bigger toy boat, and if Captain Van Pelt shows me some things, maybe I can have her win the race."

"I'm going to race mine with the little boys," decided Freddie.

The next few days were filled with fun which the Bobbsey twins very much enjoyed. They liked Storm Haven almost better than any other place where they had spent a summer vacation.

Captain Van Pelt called at Buttonball Cottage early one morning toward the end of the week, and spoke to Mrs. Bobbsey.

"I promised your children a sail on my schooner when she was all repaired," said the seaman. "Well, she's in fine shape now. Most of my crew is back on board. If you'll allow me, I'd like to take the boys and girls on a little voyage."

"That would be lovely of you, Captain," said Mrs. Bobbsey. "But you won't keep them out too long, will you?"

"Oh, no. I'll have 'em back by night unless we're storm-bound," he promised with a laugh.

"Oh, you don't think there'll be a storm, do you?"

"No, I don't," said the captain, looking up at the sky. "Of course, you never can tell about the weather, but the *Debby D* is a staunch sailing vessel. I'll take good care of your children."

You can imagine how delighted Bert and the

others were when told that they might make a little trip with Captain Van Pelt.

"Maybe we'll be shipwrecked!" whispered Freddie.

"If we are I hope it's on an island with cocoanuts and oranges," said Flossie.

"Not much chance of that around here," laughed Bert.

Once more they were rowed out to the craft by Pegleg Baldwin.

"All aboard!" called Captain Van Pelt as he stood on the deck. "Up with the anchor, men!"

Several sailors were on the schooner, and they ran about getting up the anchor and making the sails ready to be hoisted.

"Yo, ho! Yo, ho! Yo, ho!" yelled Mr. Green, flapping his gay wings.

Up came the anchor. The wind blew on the sails. The Bobbsey twins were off on a little voyage!

CHAPTER IV

A LOST FAMILY

STARTING slowly at first under the gentle breeze blowing across the harbor of Storm Haven, the schooner, with the Bobbsey twins aboard, began to slip through the water. Gradually it gained speed, the sails puffed out under the stronger wind, and the little summer resort village on the beach began to recede.

"Why, we're going right out to sea!" exclaimed Nan, seeing the big waves. She was standing with Bert near the wheel by which Captain Van Pelt was steering his craft.

"Yes," said the captain, "we're going outside the harbor, my lass. Right out into the open ocean. That's the only place I can properly try my boat since I've had the repairs made. But you aren't afraid, are you?"

"Of course we aren't!" declared Bert.

"We've been on short ocean trips before," Nan explained.

"We were on the deep, blue sea," added Freddie, rather proudly.

"Were you, indeed?" asked the captain.

"We went all the way to Florida," added Flossie, "and I hardly got sick at all when the waves got big."

"That's fine!" said the captain. "It's no fun to be seasick. I'm glad you're all good sailors. It isn't likely that we'll have any rough water on this little trip. I'm going to sail down the coast a short distance and then turn back. If my schooner acts well I'll go on a long trip later and get your father another load of lumber."

"And will you come back to Storm Haven again?" asked Freddie.

"I hope so," answered the captain who, now that the ship was well under way, turned the steering wheel over to one of his men. "I didn't find what I was looking for here," he went on with that same air of sadness Nan and Bert had noticed about him before, "so I have no real reason for coming back. But do you want me to, my little man?"

"Yes," Freddie answered, "I thought maybe you might want to see me race my little ship. Bert is going to get a bigger toy boat and race that."

"Well, then I guess I'll be back," said the captain with a laugh. "I shouldn't want to miss those races."

"I'll be glad to have you show me how to rig my new craft, if it needs it, after I get it," said Bert. "I have to save some money for it first, though. Those big playthings cost a lot."

"Yes, but some of them are very nicely made," said Captain Van Pelt. "Well, my lad, I'll help you all I can. But as I said before, I didn't find what I was looking for at Storm Haven."

"That's too bad," murmured Nan.

"Yes," agreed the captain. "But I may have better luck in some other place. Do you mind sitting on my lap a little while?" he asked Flossie.

"I like to sit in laps and listen to stories," said Flossie with a laugh. She was already great friends with Captain Van Pelt, as were all the Bobbsey twins.

"Well, I don't know that I'll have time to tell you one now," went on the sailor. "I'm going to be very busy watching how my schooner behaves since it has been repaired. I may have to jump up at any time if something seems to be going wrong. But some day I'll have time to tell you a story. Come here and let me hold you."

He sat down on a small keg near the companionway stairs that led down into his cabin. Flossie climbed up on his knee and cuddled down. Freddie was feeding Mr. Green bits of cracker Pegleg Baldwin had given him for the parrot. Bert and Nan were looking over the schooner rail at the blue sea, which seemed to be slipping past them rapidly.

"I guess you're wondering why I've taken such a liking to Flossie, my dears," said the captain to the other Bobbsey twins as they gathered about him. "Well, I'll tell you. It has to do with my secret and is part of a mystery."

"Oh, now I'm going to find out!" thought Nan.

"The reason I've taken such a liking to Flossie," went on the sailor, "is that I sort of think of her as my own little daughter."

"Did you have a little girl like me once?" asked Flossie.

"Yes, I did, my dear. She had blue eyes and golden curls like yours. She looked like my wife."

"Where is she now?" asked Freddie, who had given Mr. Green all the crackers. The parrot was yelling "More! More!" But he did not get any.

"My little daughter is lost, and so is my wife," went on Captain Van Pelt. "My entire family is lost to me."

"Oh, that's too bad!" exclaimed Nan. No wonder poor Captain Van Pelt looked so sad, she thought. And was this the mystery?

"How did it happen?" asked Bert.

"Well, it isn't a very long story, though it took many years to happen, and the end isn't yet," said the sailor. "I may as well tell you everything. Then you might be able to aid me. I ask everybody I meet to help me find my lost wife and daughter," he said in a low voice. "Even you children might solve the mystery."

"Then it's a mystery?" asked Bert.

"Yes, in a way it is, my lad."

"We'll help you all we can," spoke Nan softly.

"I was pretty sure you would," murmured the old man. Even though he was spry and lively, as are most sailors, Captain Van Pelt was rather old and had gray hair.

He reached into an inner coat pocket and took out three photographs. One was that of a young man, another that of a lady, while the third disclosed the features of a little girl about seven years old. She looked something like Flossie, and she had very fluffy hair like hers. Of course, in the photograph the golden color did not show, nor did the blue eyes.

"That was my family when I was a young man," said Captain Van Pelt. "There I am when I first went sailing," and he pointed to the picture. "No use looking at that." He put it back into his pocket. "I'm not lost. I'm here, but my wife," and he pointed to the photograph, "is missing—lost— so is my little girl. They are both gone—all the family I ever had—and I'd give the world to find them."

"How did they get lost?" asked Bert. "Were they shipwrecked?"

"No, my boy, but I was. That's the story. I was shipwrecked, and when I was rescued and got back to my home in New England after many years, my wife had moved away. I couldn't find a trace of her. She had taken my little girl with her, thinking I would never come back, I suppose, and from that day to this I've never been able to find them. Where they went is indeed a sad mystery."

"How did you get shipwrecked?" asked Bert.

"Well, it was during a storm. You see, all my people followed the sea. I went as a sailor when I was old enough. Then I got married, and for seven years, after the time my little girl was born, I didn't go on very long trips—just up and down the coast as I do now.

"But when my child was about seven years old I had a chance to go on a journey to Australia. I went, though I felt bad about leaving my wife and little girl behind. It was on that voyage in the tropical seas that the ship was wrecked in a bad storm. She broke up. I managed to cling to a bit of wreckage and was washed ashore on what might be called a desert island.

"It wasn't exactly barren, though, for things to eat grew there. Besides, there were birds, turtles, goats, and other animals. I managed, like Robinson Crusoe, to build myself a hut. There I lived for several years, always looking for a ship to come near enough so that somebody might see my distress signals and take me home. At last one did come and I managed to get back to New England. I hastened to the place where I used to reside, but strange people were living in my old home. My wife and little girl were gone, no one knew where. You see, we didn't have any relatives to whom I could go for any information as to their whereabouts. So that's how my family was lost to me."

"It's too bad," said Bert.

"Do you think your wife and little girl are alive now?" asked Nan softly.

"I don't know. It's hard to say. This happened

many years ago. If my wife is alive she would be about my age. And if my daughter is living, she is probably married. That would cause her to change her name and I shouldn't know how to go about finding her. That's what makes it so hard for me."

"What was your little girl's name?" asked Nan.

"Deborah," came the answer, "but we always called her Debby. My schooner is named after her, the *Debby D.*"

"Is 'D' the initial of your daughter's last name?" asked Bert.

"I couldn't say," answered Captain Van Pelt. "I don't know what her name might be, assuming she is married. I just picked out the letter 'D' without any real reason. I liked the sound of it.

"Well, that's my story, and a sad and mysterious one it is. Every place I go to that's near the sea, I go ashore and make inquiries trying to find my lost family. I have a notion that my wife, if she is alive, and my daughter, even though she may be married and have children of her own, will always live near the sea. That's why I came to Storm Haven—to find out about them. But it has been of no use. Nobody here knows anything about my lost family."

CHAPTER V

THE TATTOOED MAN

Captain van pelt remained silent a few moments after he had finished telling his sad, mysterious story. So did the Bobbsey twins. Everyone was deep in thought as the schooner sailed on and on.

Finally Nan remarked:

"We feel very sorry for you, and if we can help you we will."

"Sure!" echoed Bert.

"I thought you would," said the captain. "I don't know if there is much you can do. But if you should hear of a middle-aged woman with a daughter, and they happen to have a sailor relative who went to sea but didn't return, just let me know about them. I'll look them up and see if they might possibly be my relatives. You can send word to me through your father," he added to Nan and Bert. "I'll always be more or less in touch with him on account of bringing him shiploads of lumber."

"We won't forget," promised Bert.

"Every place we go where we think it might do any good," added Nan, "we'll ask about it."

"Thank you, my dear. And now enough of sadness. I must go see what the cook plans to give us for lunch."

"Oh, are we going to eat on your ship?" asked Flossie in delight.

"Of course, my dear," said the captain. "You're on an all-day voyage with me, and you're to be my guests at luncheon."

"Will it be like a party?" asked Freddie.

"Well, you might call it that!" chuckled the captain. "But I can't promise you ice cream."

"Oh, we've been to parties before where there wasn't any ice cream," said Flossie.

"Most always they have cake," spoke Freddie.

"Well, I think I can promise you cake all right," laughed Captain Van Pelt.

While he was below making sure the cook would have a cake for the children, Bert and the others wandered about the deck of the *Debby D*. They were interested not only in the new things they saw, and amused by the funny sayings of the parrot, but the older twins especially were thinking about the captain's story.

In their walk about the deck the children saw
Pegleg Baldwin, who was working near one of the
masts. His big brown hands, with red and blue
tattoo marks of anchors, palm trees and strange
designs, were busy with many ropes.

"How do you like it, messmates?" he asked in
his deep voice.

"It's a nice ship," said Flossie.

"Do you have those marks all over you?" asked
Freddie, pointing to the tattooing.

"Pretty much, messmates, pretty much," answered Pegleg. "I'm quite well tattooed. That is,
all but my wooden leg," he added with a laugh.
"No use tattooing that. It wears out and I have
to get a new one now and then. But outside of that
I'm pretty well covered. Would you like to see a
whale?" he asked suddenly.

"Do you mean a real one?" asked Nan, looking
over the waves.

"No, little miss, I mean a tattooed one."

"Please show us!" begged Bert.

Pegleg Baldwin rolled up the shirt sleeve of his
left arm. Just above the wrist there was tattooed a
big, blue whale, spouting water.

"Oh-ee-ee!" squealed Flossie. "He's wonderful!"

"What's on your other arm?" asked Freddie.

"A shark," said the old sailor. "Like to see him?"

Pegleg rolled up his other sleeve. There was revealed a big shark done in red ink, and the ink was pricked with needles below the skin of the sailor's arm so the marks would never wash off. Tattooing stays on forever.

"That's fine," said Freddie. "Could you tattoo a shark on me, Mr. Pegleg?"

"Freddie Bobbsey, don't you dare think of such a thing!" warned Nan.

"Oh, I don't mean now," Freddie said. "I mean when I grow up to be a sailor. I first was going to be a fireman," he told Mr. Baldwin. "But now I guess I'll be a tattooed sailor."

"Well, you might do worse!" chuckled the old salt.

There was so much to interest the Bobbsey twins aboard the *Debby D,* that almost before they knew it they heard eight tinkles of a bell. There were four strokes of two taps each.

"Eight bells!" exclaimed Bert, who remembered this from another sea voyage he had made. "That means it's twelve o'clock."

"Then it's time to eat!" exclaimed Flossie.

And it was. Presently Captain Van Pelt came

up on deck to say that lunch was ready in his cabin.

Even though it was not exactly a party and there was not any ice cream, it was nevertheless a jolly occasion for the twins. And there was a great big chocolate cake which the cook passed around.

The children were resting in the cabin after the meal, and Captain Van Pelt had gone to see about one of the sails, when Bert and Nan noticed that the ship was pitching and tossing much more than it had at any time since they had come aboard.

"We must be getting farther out to sea," Bert said.

"I hope we don't go out too far," murmured Nan.

They could hear on the deck above them the hurried tramp of feet and the shouting of orders. The ship rolled, pitched and tossed more violently. Pegleg Baldwin came stumping down into the cabin.

"Is anything the matter?" asked Bert.

"We've run into a pretty bad storm," said the tattooed sailor. "We may not be able to get back to Storm Haven tonight. It's a bad gale and growing worse."

CHAPTER VI

IN A STORM

THE Bobbsey twins were startled greatly by this announcement.

"Is the wind blowing very hard?" asked Bert, for the old sailor seemed to have some difficulty in closing the cabin door.

"Yes, it's blowing quite a gale," he answered.

"It must be raining, too," added Nan. "You're all wet."

"Part of my wetness is from rain," answered Pegleg, "but most of it came from the spray that's blowing aboard. The sea is running pretty high now, and we have to head right into the storm. That's why the captain can't turn about and sail for Storm Haven. He's afraid to trust the ship, newly repaired as she is."

"Then what's to be done?" asked Bert.

"We'll just have to keep heading into the storm as best we can," said the tattooed sailor. "If we turn and run before it we may not be able to make

Storm Haven harbor. And it's safer water down here below Storm Haven than it is above it. We'd have to go up there if we changed our course. We may have to keep into the storm all night."

"Can't we go home?" asked Flossie.

"I don't see how you can," was the answer. "But don't be afraid. If you're a brave little girl I'll show you a swan tattooed on the back of my neck," and Pegleg Baldwin began to loosen his collar.

"I'm not afraid to stay on this ship all night," boasted Freddie. "And I'm sure Flossie will be a brave girl 'cause I want to see that tattooed swan." he said.

"Sure I'll be brave!" promised Flossie. "Will we have our supper on this boat?"

"Of course, and breakfast, too!" laughed Mr. Baldwin, as he braced himself against the lurching of the ship. "Look here, my dears!"

He now had his collar open, and in the faint light that came through the storm-dimmed ports of the cabin the children saw a red swan with blue wings tattooed on the brown neck of the old wooden-legged seaman.

"It's funny!" said Flossie.

"Have you any more animals on you?" asked

Freddie. He thought Pegleg belonged in a zoo.

"I've a green lion on my chest," said Pegleg. "I'll show that to you some other time. Just now the captain sent me down to make sure you were all right. I'm going to make a light, for it will soon be dark here with the storm coming on."

He lighted a kerosene lamp which hung from the ceiling. It cast a pleasant glow about the cabin, making strange shadows as it swung to and fro because of the tossing of the schooner.

"What do you suppose Mother will say when we don't come back?" asked Nan of Bert.

"I don't believe she'll worry much," he answered. "When she said Captain Van Pelt could take us on this little voyage he told her we might run into bad weather and have to stay out all night. Of course, he didn't really expect that would happen, but since he did speak of it, I think Mother won't worry."

"I hope not," murmured Nan. "Anyhow, it can't be helped. We shan't be able to get back home until the storm stops in the morning."

"I think it's fun here," stated Flossie.

"But where are we going to sleep?" asked Freddie. "I don't see any beds."

"I guess there are bunks in some of these rooms

that open from this cabin," suggested Bert. He pointed to several doors around the walls of the main cabin, which held a desk, a table, and some chairs, all fastened to the floor so they would not move about when the schooner pitched and tossed in the storm.

"I wish I knew where we were going to sleep," suggested Flossie. "Let's look in some of these rooms, if we can open the doors."

"Maybe we'd better wait until Captain Van Pelt comes down," suggested Nan.

"Oh, I don't believe he'd mind," said Bert. "He said for us to make ourselves at home on his ship."

Pegleg Baldwin had gone up on deck again. The tramping of many feet could be heard, as well as the shouts of Captain Van Pelt and his sailor crew.

Flossie and Freddie had found an illustrated Sunday newspaper and were looking at the funny sheet. Bert and Nan were debating whether or not to look in the rooms about the main cabin.

"Well, here goes, anyhow!" exclaimed Bert after a while. "I'll try this door."

It was a sliding one, the kind used on ships because they take up less room than swinging doors. No sooner had Bert touched the knob than a voice from within the room shouted:

"Get away from that door! Don't you dare come in! Let me alone!"

Bert jumped back in surprise. Nan started to run. Then she began to laugh.

"It's only Mr. Green, the parrot," said Nan.

"That's so!" chuckled Bert. "At first I thought it was a real person."

"So did I," admitted Nan. "Go on, open the door."

Bert did so. He found a room with two berths in it. The parrot's cage was hanging from a hook on the side, and was swaying to and fro with the motion of the ship.

"Well, some of us could sleep in there if they would take Mr. Green out," Nan said, as the light from the lamp in the main cabin revealed the bunks. "I suppose I'd better sleep with Flossie. You can take Freddie if there's another room with two bunks."

"I guess there will be," Bert said. "We'll have a look."

He opened a second door, showing a room, which also had two berths in it. There seemed to be plenty of cabin sleeping quarters on the *Debby D*. The crew, of course, slept forward in the "focas'le," as it is called.

Having made sure there would be beds for them and the younger twins, Nan and Bert sat down in the cabin to wait for Captain Van Pelt. They thought he would come below to see them, once he was sure the schooner was riding well in the storm.

"I think this is fun," remarked Bert, while Flossie and Freddie were still looking at the comic paper.

"So do I," said Nan. "We didn't think we'd have such an adventure as being out at sea in a storm when we came to this place, did we?"

"I'll say we didn't!" exclaimed Bert.

"And wouldn't it be wonderful," went on Nan. "if we could solve the mystery and find Captain Van Pelt's missing daughter?"

"It would," Bert agreed, "but I don't see how we can. Still, we have had pretty good luck in other adventures, and we may in this one, too."

The storm was growing worse. Not only rain, but salty spray from the big waves outside dashed against the thick glass of the ports of the cabin.

Suddenly, while Bert and Nan were sitting on either side of the table, the door of one of the little bunk rooms into which the twins had not looked, slid back. From the room there stepped a strange figure. It was that of a young woman wearing the clothes of a man—a short coat and wide trousers. She looked at the children in surprise, blinking her eyes as if she had just awakened.

"My goodness! Where am I? Who are you?" she asked.

CHAPTER VII

OVERBOARD

NAN was the first one to answer the strange young woman in men's clothing.

"We're the Bobbsey twins. Who are you?"

"Well," said the young lady with a laugh, "I guess I'm a stowaway, though I didn't mean to be. Oh, are we in a storm?"

"Yes, we are," replied Bert. "A bad one."

"Oh, what a mess!" exclaimed the stranger.

"What did you say you were?" asked Nan, not sure she had heard aright, for the storm was making such loud, booming sounds.

"I guess I'm a stowaway on this schooner, whatever its name is," was the answer. "I didn't take the trouble to look when I came aboard."

"This is the *Debby D*," remarked Nan. "Does the captain know you are here?"

"Of course he doesn't!" exclaimed Bert. "She wouldn't be a stowaway if the captain knew she was here."

"Oh," said Nan meekly. She hoped that the stowaway would not feel bad about her plight.

"Your brother is right," went on the young woman. "A stowaway is a person who hides on a ship with the hope of getting a free ride. I didn't exactly do that, but I'm a stowaway nevertheless, for I am getting a free ride though I didn't really want it. I'd be a stowaway just the same if I hid away on an airship or in a balloon."

"I was in a balloon once," said Freddie. "It was at the county fair."

"That was nice," said the stowaway. "Let me see now, what shall I do next?"

"She talks like a school teacher," whispered Nan to Bert, and a little later they were surprised to find that Nan had guessed correctly.

"Can you tell me, Bobbsey twins," asked the stowaway, "where this vessel is bound for?"

"Just down the coast a little ways," Bert answered. "We came to have a ride, and were to be back in Storm Haven by night. But when the storm came up Pegleg Baldwin said we couldn't turn back. So we're riding out the storm and maybe we won't get back until morning."

"Well, as long as I can return to Storm Haven by morning I suppose it will be all right," said the young woman, who did not seem to think it at all strange that she should be wearing boys' clothes. "Is Pegleg Baldwin the captain?" she asked.

"Oh, no," said Flossie with a laugh. "He's a sailor with a wooden leg and he's all bambooed."

"Tattooed! Tattooed!" corrected Bert with a laugh.

"And he has a green lion on his chest," added Flossie, "and he'll show it to you if you're a brave girl!"

"Will he? That's fine!" laughed the stowaway. "But I wish I could meet the captain and explain to him that I didn't really mean to hide away on his ship."

There was a noise at the main door of the cabin —a noise that could be heard above the storm, and Captain Van Pelt, with water dripping from him, entered.

"Well, well!" he exclaimed, plainly surprised at the sight of the young woman wearing trousers and a coat. "Is this some friend of yours, Bobbsey twins?"

"She's a stowaway!" exclaimed Freddie.

"I'm afraid that's what I am," admitted the strange passenger. "Perhaps I'd better explain."

"Maybe you had," said the captain, taking off

his yellow oilskin coat and laying aside his big sou'wester hat. "Please have a chair—er—miss— I reckon you're a miss, though you look like a boy."

"Yes, I am Sarah Perkin," was the answer. "I live out near Portchester," naming a city several miles away. "I teach school there. Not in clothes like these, though," she said quickly. "I taught up to the time of the summer vacation. Because of the hard times, we teachers didn't get paid so I de- cided to try earning some money this vacation. I came to Storm Haven where I've been told there are many fishing clubs. But I had no luck getting work."

"What sort of work were ye looking for?" asked Captain Van Pelt.

"I'm an expert fly-caster," was the answer. "My father taught me when I was a little girl, and I've kept it up. I have won many contests along the Atlantic coast. I thought I might be able to give lessons in fly-casting here and earn some money that way."

"And you didn't have any luck?" asked the cap- tain.

"None to speak of. I wear these clothes, as it's easier for me to do fly-casting in them than in a skirt. I am boarding in Storm Haven, but I'm afraid I can't stay there much longer. My money is almost gone, and nobody seems to want to learn fly-casting."

"I'd like to learn how to catch flies," said Freddie.

"Oh, you little dear, fly-casting isn't exactly catching flies, though you do use something on your pole and line that is called a fly," said Miss Perkin with a laugh. "You see," she went on, with the school-teacher air Nan had noticed, "many fishermen don't like to catch fish by just putting a worm or a grasshopper on the hook. They like to make an art of it by fastening onto their hooks a bunch of feathers or wool made to look like a brilliant fly or insect.

"This artificial fly they throw out over a lake, pond, river, or even the ocean, and in that way they may get a fish on the hook. That's what I learned from my father—how to cast a light fly a considerable distance, and to land one inside a barrel hoop nearly every time. You see, a fly-caster must not only toss his hook a long way but he must make it land in a certain spot. As I said, nobody here seems to want to take lessons from me."

"Oh," said Freddie. He had hoped to help. Now

it did not seem very likely. He really felt sorry for the pleasant lady.

"I thought she said fly-catcher, too," whispered Flossie to her small brother.

They went back to their picture paper, no longer interested now that there was no opportunity of catching flies. Captain Van Pelt asked:

"Did you board my schooner, Miss Perkin, with the idea of teaching me to cast flies?"

"No, I didn't," she answered, still smiling. "I just happened to come on board. I didn't know what to do with myself. I was sort of sad and discouraged when I found I couldn't earn any money. So I borrowed a boat at the dock right after breakfast and rowed out into the bay. I passed this schooner. I gave a hail to ask if I might come aboard and look around. But no one answered."

"I reckon," said Captain Van Pelt, "that Pegleg Baldwin was the only one here at the time, and he very likely was below. He didn't hear you. The crew didn't come aboard until later, and then I followed with the Bobbsey twins."

"Well, no one answered me," said Miss Perkin. "So I just fastened my boat to the platform of the accommodation ladder and came on board. Still I saw no one. I came down to this cabin. I noticed a comfortable bunk in one of the rooms, so I was daring enough to lie down to rest.

"I was very, very tired, for I hadn't rested all last night on account of worrying about what I was going to do. I must have fallen fast asleep. The next thing I knew I heard voices, and felt the ship in motion. Then I came out and saw these children. That's my story."

"And a strange one it is!" laughed Captain Van Pelt. "I don't blame you a bit. You're quite welcome to stay here until we get back to Storm Haven with the Bobbsey twins. I expect that will be tomorrow morning. It's too bad you couldn't get anybody to take fly-casting lessons."

"Yes, it was disappointing. But perhaps in the fall, when I have to go back to teaching school, times will be better and we teachers will get paid."

"I hope so," murmured Nan, who was beginning to admire Miss Perkin.

"Thank you, my dear," said the stowaway. "And now," she added to the captain, "if you want me to work for my passage, which I understand stowaways always must do, just show me what to do. I'll make beds or peel potatoes."

"Well, thank you kindly, miss," chuckled the captain, "but the cook has the potatoes all peeled,

I expect. Since you and the children have to stay on board tonight it might be a good idea for you to look after the bunks."

"I'll do that."

"And I'll help!" exclaimed Nan. "I'd love to."

"Are we going to have supper?" asked Freddie.

"I'm hungry, too!" voiced Flossie.

"If you sniff right hearty," said the captain, "you will smell the supper cooking on the galley stove right now. I must go up on deck again but I'll be down in time for supper."

"May we go up and have a look at the storm before it gets too dark?" asked Miss Perkin.

"Well, I don't mind you and Bert coming on deck," was the answer, "but I'm afraid it's too rough and stormy for Nan and the two little ones. They'd better stay below."

"Yes, indeed," Nan agreed.

"I'd like to go up," said Bert.

"All right," agreed the captain. "You'd better put on oilskins," he added, "both of you. You'll find some in that locker," and he pointed to a sort of closet in one corner of the cabin. "There're two small suits that former cabin boys I had used. They'll about fit you and Bert, Miss Perkin. Without 'em you'll be drenched."

"Thanks," said the stowaway. "Bert and I will be up as soon as the berths are made ready."

It did not take her and Nan long to arrange the sheets, pillow cases and blankets on the shelf-like beds. Then, after Bert had donned the yellow water-proof garment and the stowaway had done the same, the two went up on deck.

It was rapidly getting dark, but there was light enough to show an angry sea with big waves. It was raining hard, and the wind was blowing.

"Oh, I love this!" cried Miss Perkin, clinging to the rail as Bert was doing.

"It's quite a storm!" he shouted back.

Suddenly the schooner gave a harder lurch than usual. The next moment Bert saw Miss Perkin slide along the rail, loose her hold, and then pitch over into a stormy sea.

"Overboard!" yelled Bert with all his might. "Man overboard! I mean a lady!" he corrected. "Overboard! Overboard!"

CHAPTER VIII

THE RESCUE

BERT BOBBSEY heard Captain Van Pelt and some sailors shouting and rushing over to where he stood. Near him on the deck was a white canvas life ring attached to a long rope. In another instant Bert had pulled this loose from the place at which it was lightly tied to the rail, and tossed it over to where he could see Miss Perkin floating amid a smother of white foam!

"What happened? What's the matter?" demanded Captain Van Pelt, as he reached the boy's side.

"She fell overboard!" the boy answered.

"Who?" asked one of the sailors.

"The stowaway! Miss Perkin! There she is now! She's near the life ring I threw!" shouted Bert.

So great was the noise of the storm that the boy's first warning cry, though it had been heard by Captain Van Pelt and others on deck, had not

been understood. Now they realized the serious-
ness of the situation.

"Lower a boat!" cried the commander to some
of his sailors. "Heave over another ring! You'll
find some on the port side," he added.

Several sailors hurried to where a small life-
boat hung on the davits, those curved pieces of
iron at the sides of most ships. The ropes, holding
the boat suspended as in a swing, were loosed,
and the little craft began to drop toward the heav-
ing billows.

No sooner had it touched the waves, bobbing
up and down on them, than three sailors slid down
the ropes and dropped into the craft. In a moment they had the oars out and were rowing
toward the floating stowaway, who had managed
to get rid of the heavy oilskin garment. Otherwise,
she might have sunk.

Bert, looking over the side, saw that Miss Perkin was a strong and expert swimmer. She was
heading toward the ring he had thrown to her.

"If she gets it," thought Bert, "maybe I can
pull her up on deck and save her." He did not
stop to think that Miss Perkin was too heavy for
him to lift, especially when wearing wet clothes.

As the boat was being rowed toward the struggling young woman, another life ring was tossed to her. But the sailor who threw it was so excited that he missed his aim, and it went wide of its mark. Bert saw that Miss Perkin would have no chance of reaching it. But now she had grasped his and was clinging to it.

"Take her in!" cried Captain Van Pelt to the rowing sailors. "Lively now, my hearties! Then bring the boat alongside and we'll hoist you all on deck!"

The boat was now close to Miss Perkin, and in a few moments she had been helped over the side. Then, rowing hard against the storm, the little craft put back to the schooner. On deck a rope was lowered, and when it was made fast about the wet body of the stowaway she was safely pulled up beside Captain Van Pelt and Bert.

"Well, so you didn't like riding with me and started to swim away on your own account, did you?" asked the commander, shouting loud enough to be heard above the roar of the wind.

"It was all—all an—accident!" panted Miss Perkin. "I—I was standing near Bert—when—all of a sudden—the ship gave a lurch and I—I went overboard!"

"Yes, that's how it happened," added Bert.

"Lucky you didn't go over, my boy!" said the captain. "Now get below, both of you. I'm sorry I have no dry clothes for you," he said to Miss Perkin, "but ladies have never traveled on my craft before."

"Oh, I'll not get dressed again after my bath," she said with a laugh. "I'll just get right into bed. And if there's a fire where my clothes might be dried——"

"I'll have the cook dry 'em in the galley," interrupted the captain. "Now get below, both of you. I shouldn't have let you come on deck in such a storm. I didn't realize how dangerous it was. Go below!"

This Bert and Miss Perkin did, and when Nan and the other children heard what had happened they were greatly excited.

"You look just as if you had been at a fire and the hose had burst," commented Freddie, looking at the dripping stowaway.

"I shouldn't mind being near a fire for a little while," she said with a laugh. "It was chilly in the water."

However, a cup of hot coffee which the cook brought to the cabin warmed and strengthened the teacher. Then Miss Perkin took off her wet garments and got into a bunk next to the little stateroom where Nan was going to sleep with Flossie. Nan took the stowaway's wet garments to the ship's kitchen to dry near the fire.

"We have had quite an adventure," said Miss Perkin at supper time later. "I hope tomorrow will be sunny and warm so the end of the trip will be nice. I must not forget to thank the sailors who saved me. And you, too, Bert. If you hadn't thrown that life ring when you did, I don't know what might have happened."

"Oh, it wasn't anything," said Bert modestly. "I just did it."

"Bert's quick!" said Freddie.

"Indeed he is," agreed the stowaway.

As the night wore on the storm seemed to lessen. Freddie and Flossie were soon asleep, one with Nan and the other with Bert. The older twins were wakeful, as was Miss Perkin, who lay worrying about what she was going to do to earn some money. If she could only get the amount due her for teaching school she would be all right. But there was no telling when the Board of Education in the town where she taught would settle with the teachers.

"Well," thought the worried stowaway, "perhaps after this storm I'll have better luck. I hope so, anyhow."

At last sleep came to all the voyagers. When morning dawned the sun was shining brightly and the storm was a thing of the past. There was still a rough sea, but the Bobbseys were good sailors, and neither they nor Miss Perkin showed any signs of illness after the experience of the day before.

"I wonder if I'll get any breakfast?" wondered Miss Perkin as they all sat in the cabin.

"Of course you will!" declared Nan. "What makes you think you won't?"

"Well, you know stowaways are supposed to work for their food and passage. I told Captain Van Pelt I'd be willing to, but he said there was nothing I could do. He's been very kind to me."

"Captain Van Pelt is a fine man!" declared Bert. "He's going to show me how to sail boats."

Suddenly through the cabin there sounded a cry.

"Help! Help! Man overboard!" shrieked the voice.

"My goodness!" exclaimed Miss Perkin, jumping up off the chair where she had been sitting "Another accident!"

But the words of alarm were quickly followed by another cry.

"I'm all wet! I'm all wet! Give me a cracker!"

"It's Mr. Green!" said Flossie with a laugh.

"Who is Mr. Green?" asked Miss Perkin.

"The parrot," explained Nan. "It's in that stateroom."

She opened the door, and it was soon discovered that poor Mr. Green was a trifle wet. The glass window of the porthole of the room where his cage hung had not been closed tightly, and some water had sprayed in on its red, green and yellow feathers.

"You poor thing!" exclaimed Nan. "Lift him into the cabin, Bert. It's warmer here and he'll dry."

When Mr. Green found himself in the midst of company he began to entertain them with funny sayings, bits of songs and whistled choruses. He was a very clever parrot, indeed.

Miss Perkin need have had no fears about getting breakfast, for in a little while Pegleg Baldwin brought it in. There was a pot of hot coffee for the stowaway, who said it was just what she needed. There was orange juice and cereal, also, and some milk for the children.

"Just as good a breakfast as if we were at home!" declared Flossie.

"Better!" said Freddie. " 'Cause it's on a ship and I'm going to be a sailor."

Captain Van Pelt came in for his morning repast a little later to announce that the storm had blown itself out, and that the ship was turned around and was now headed back for the harbor.

"I'll land my passengers before noon," he said. "But I'll be sorry to see you go ashore. I've enjoyed your company, and yours also, ma'am," he said to the stowaway. "I'm sorry you had to fall overboard."

"Oh, I didn't *have* to!" she said with a laugh. "And I never can thank you enough for being so kind to me. I feel as if I ought to repay you in some way."

"I don't see how you can, ma'am," he said with a twinkle in his eyes. "You say you haven't any money and I wouldn't take it if you did have."

"Well, I might show my appreciation in some other way," she said.

"How?" he asked.

"Well," said Miss Perkin, "I can sing a little and I play the piano rather well. If you had a piano here I could entertain you and your crew and the children on our trip back. I often used to entertain my school children with songs and music."

"I like music as well as the next man," said Captain Van Pelt, "but we have no piano aboard the *Debby D.* My wife used to play," he said, and again the children noted the sad air about him. "But that was years ago. I'll take the will for the deed, ma'am. You don't need to feel you owe me anything. It's been a pleasure to have had you aboard."

"Thank you, Captain," answered the stowaway.

After breakfast they all went up on deck into the sunshine. Miss Perkin did not look at all strange now, the children thought, in her coat and trousers. The clothes seemed to become her very well. Nan rather wished that she might some day dress that way herself.

Under a fair wind the schooner made good time back toward Storm Haven. Captain Van Pelt announced that he was satisfied with the trial voyage his vessel had made. He found the repairs to be well done, and added that he was now ready for a long sail.

"Are you going to get more lumber for my father?" asked Bert.

"I expect to, my lad," was the reply. "I'm going to telephone him as soon as I get back to shore."

"I wish you didn't have to go away," said Bert.

"Why, son?"

"Well, I was sort of thinking that maybe I wouldn't buy myself a big toy boat," went on the Bobbsey boy. "I think I'd rather have a real craft —a small cat boat, you know. And if you could teach me how to sail her I might compete in the hotel regatta."

"Say, that's a good idea!" exclaimed the captain. "If I have time and your father approves, I'll look around to see if I can get you a small boat down here. There's nothing like knowing how to handle one, even if it has only one sail. And you can't learn too soon. I'll see what I can do."

This made Bert feel happy. Indeed, they were all in the best of spirits on that return voyage. Even Miss Perkin, in spite of her worry over money matters, was very cheerful. She sat on deck with the children and sang a few songs for them, though she said they would have sounded better if she had had a piano for an accompaniment.

The *Debby D* was within sight of the village of Storm Haven and sailing along very nicely, when

Nan looked around for Flossie. She had wandered away after Miss Perkin had finished the last song.

"I'd better go find her," Nan said.

Just then Flossie's voice was heard up forward, toward the bow of the boat.

"Quick! Come here quick!" cried the little Bobbsey girl.

Bert and Nan started to run in her direction.

CHAPTER IX

BERT'S NEW BOAT

THE older twins, having heard Flossie's excited shout, thought they would find the little girl in some kind of trouble. They soon saw she was in no danger. As they went up toward the big mast nearest the bow of the boat, they saw Flossie looking at Pegleg Baldwin, who was at work among the many ropes that seemed to be all in a tangle about the big stick to which the sail was fastened.

The wooden-legged sailor was not paying any attention to Flossie, for he was very busy with his work. It was getting near the time for the schooner to drop anchor again in the bay of Storm Haven.

"What is it, Flossie?" asked Nan.

"Yes, what were you yelling about?" Bert wanted to know.

"Look!" and this time Flossie whispered as she pointed at the sailor. "I saw it! I saw it on him!"

"Saw what on him?" asked Bert.

"The green lion that's bambooed on his chest," whispered Flossie. "His shirt is open at the neck and I could see his chest. Just as he said, it has a green lion bambooed on it."

"Tattooed you mean! Tattooed!" said Bert, laughing.

"Is that all you called us for?" asked Nan.

"Yes," her sister answered. "That's all. You know that Mr. Pegleg promised to show us the green lion if we were brave. Well, I guess I wasn't afraid, and I saw the bam—I mean tattooed lion without his showing it to me."

As she spoke, the sailor leaned over to pick up a rope. His shirt was loosely fastened around his neck, and Bert and Nan caught a glimpse of the green, tattooed lion. It was rather a strange sight. There were glimpses of other animals and designs in red and blue ink tattooed on the old sailor's body, but none showed up as plainly as did the lion.

"He must be quite a sight with his shirt off," murmured Nan.

"Like the tattooed man in the circus," agreed Bert.

By this time Pegleg Baldwin seemed to know that he was being looked at. He finished coiling a long rope, glanced up, saw the three children, and then laughed.

"Well, you caught me!" he chuckled. "And I guess you had a look at my green lion. I was going to show him to you, anyhow. Take a good look!" He stood up and bared his chest. As he breathed in and out the lion seemed to move as if alive.

"That's wonderful!" exclaimed Flossie. Then she started to run.

"Where are you going?" asked Nan.

"I'm going to call Freddie," was her answer. "He'll want to see the lion. Please don't button your shirt, Mr. Pegleg," she begged.

"All right, my little lass, I won't," was the old sailor's answer. "I'll wait for Freddie."

When the little boy had had a look at the strange sight, he was as much delighted and impressed as Flossie and the others had been.

Pegleg had to attend to some other work on the ship, so he hurried away. All the other sailors were busy in various parts of the vessel, while Captain Van Pelt was at the wheel to steer his craft to a safe anchorage not far from the big public dock at Storm Haven. Miss Perkin was ready to go ashore with the children.

"I want to thank you for being so kind to a stowaway that went aboard your ship and fell asleep," said the teacher, as she and the others were landed on the dock. "I'm afraid I caused you a lot of trouble."

"No trouble at all! None at all!" was the hearty answer. "I was glad to have you and the children for passengers. Our voyage lasted a little longer than I intended it should when I took the Bobbsey twins on board, but that was the fault of the storm. I hope your mother won't blame me," he said to Bert and Nan.

"Oh, I guess she won't," Bert answered. "I'll explain it to her."

"And I hope you find some kind of work to earn money," said the captain to Miss Perkin.

"Thank you, I hope I do," she said, as she made ready to walk down the shore road to the cottage where she boarded.

"Maybe you could catch some flies at our house," suggested Freddie, as he and his brother and sisters said good-bye to Miss Perkin.

"Fly-casting, not fly catching!" whispered Bert.

"Oh, well," said Freddie, as the school teacher stowaway walked off, "it would be a good thing to catch flies anyhow."

"I'll see you children again, I hope," spoke Captain Van Pelt as he started for the hotel, while the Bobbsey twins turned off in the direction of Buttonball Cottage. "I don't know just how long I'll be here now that my ship is repaired. It will depend on what your father wants me to do about a lumber cargo. But if I have to go away in a hurry I'll be back again, I'm sure."

"And if we can find out anything about your wife or your little girl that you lost track of so long ago," said Nan, "we'll let you know."

"Thank you, my lass. I'll be glad to have you try to solve the mystery for me," answered the sailor.

"And I hope," said Bert, "that you'll have a chance to teach me something about sailing a cat boat."

"I will!" promised Captain Van Pelt.

"Why, Bert!" exclaimed Nan, "you aren't going to have a cat boat, are you? Do you mean a real sailboat that you can get in and sail and steer yourself?"

"Sure I do!" declared Bert. "I think I'm too big to be playing with or racing toy boats even if they are bigger than Freddie's. I'm going to get a real boat if Daddy will let me."

The children were soon at the cottage. They found their mother anxiously waiting for them. She had been worried, naturally, but when they did not come home as night drew on and the storm came up, she felt they would be safe aboard the schooner with Captain Van Pelt. A neighbor who had marine glasses had looked out into the harbor just a little while before the Bobbsey twins had landed, and had reported that the *Debby D* was on her way back to her anchorage.

"It was quite an adventure, my dears," she said, as she kissed Flossie and Freddie, "being out in a storm like that."

Late that afternoon Captain Van Pelt came to Buttonball Cottage to say that he had talked with Mr. Bobbsey in Lakeport over the telephone.

"He isn't certain just when I'll have to go after another load of lumber for him," said the sailor, "so I may be here longer than I thought. Your husband told me, Mrs. Bobbsey," he said, "that he would be here tomorrow. He asked me, since I was in the neighborhood, to give you his message."

"Then I can ask him about my boat!" said Bert, his eyes shining with delight at the prospect.

Of course, when Mr. Bobbsey arrived at Buttonball Cottage next day he had to hear all about the voyage, the stowaway, the parrot, and the green lion on the chest of Pegleg Baldwin. Then Bert found a chance to ask his father if he might have a small boat, and have Captain Van Pelt teach him something about sailing.

"Why, that isn't a bad idea, Bert," answered Mr. Bobbsey. "I rather like it. A boy should know how to sail a boat. I'll talk to the captain about it. I have to see him this afternoon anyway."

Bert was not present when his father and Captain Van Pelt had a talk. But the next day, after Mr. Bobbsey had gone back to Lakeport, the captain paid another visit to Buttonball Cottage. Calling to Bert, he said:

"If you'll come with me, my hearty, you may see something that will please you."

"Is it my boat?" asked Bert eagerly.

"Well, not to keep you guessing, it is, yes," was the answer. "Your father told me to be on the lookout for a small cat boat that didn't cost too much. So I found one and I've bought it for you. She's over at Jason's dock. We'll go there and take a look at her."

It was only a short walk to the place. There Bert found, moored to the float, a small cat boat. It had a centreboard and was roomy enough to hold four passengers. There was a broad seat in the stern where the steersman sat to handle the helm and also the "sheet." Bert was rather surprised to learn that the "sheet" was the name of a rope, and not that of a large piece of white cloth.

"Sailors have queer names for things," Captain Van Pelt said when Bert remarked this. "But you want to mind both your helm and your sheet, for by the 'sheet' you manage the main sail."

"Oh," said Bert.

"Now I'll take you out on your boat and give you a few lessons," said the old seaman.

"Is it really my boat?" asked Bert.

"Yes," was the answer, "it is. Your name's not on it, for it was christened *Fairy*, but if you like I'll have one of my men change it."

"No, thank you," said Bert, thinking it over. "I'll keep the name *Fairy*. That's what my father used to call Flossie."

"Ah, she's a fine little girl!" sighed Captain Van Pelt. "I wish I knew where my daughter, who once looked like your sister Flossie, might be. I'd like to see her. But I guess I never shall. Don't mind me, though. Get in your boat, Bert, and we'll go sailing."

Bert Bobbsey found there was more to learn about sailing even a small cat boat than he had ever imagined. It was so easy to do something wrong. But Captain Van Pelt was a good sailor. He was also a clever and painstaking teacher.

He showed Bert how to sit properly in the stern seat, regulate the tiller in the right way to keep the craft's sail filled with wind, and how to hold the sheet so it would not tangle.

"While we're about it," went on the old man, "I want to show you how to bring a sailboat up to the wharf at the end of a voyage. More people make mistakes that way than any other. They try to come up to a dock with the wind at the back instead of in the face. You must make port into or against the wind, not with it."

Bert felt a great thrill of delight when he could hold the rope of the sail in one hand, and could feel the wind blowing on the canvas as though it wanted to pull it away from him. The *Fairy* glided along with the breeze, tilting a little to one side as the winds freshened.

"Mind your helm!" suddenly called Captain Van Pelt.

"What's the matter?" asked Bert.

"You're spilling the wind," was the answer.

"How did I spill the wind?" asked Bert, changing the direction of the *Fairy* as the sail puffed out more.

"Oh, you were sailing what is known as too 'close'," was the seaman's reply. "While you are learning you want to keep your sail as full of wind as you can. It's easier that way. After you get to be an expert you can do differently."

It was all a bit puzzling to Bert, but he paid strict attention to what Captain Van Pelt told him.

"Well, I guess this will be enough for one time," said the sailor after a while. "If you try to learn too much at the beginning you may forget half of it. I'll take the boat back to the dock, and you watch how I do it."

He changed places with the captain, who took charge of the tiller and sheet. As they were headed back for shore Mr. Van Pelt asked:

"Who owns that small wharf near your cottage, Bert?" and he pointed to one built out into the bay.

"It belongs to Mr. Hanson," was the reply. "He owns Buttonball Cottage too, I heard my mother say."

"Then he ought to be willing to let you land the *Fairy* there," said the captain.

Mr. Hanson was very willing that Bert should use his dock. So the little cat boat was anchored there.

"And now," said Captain Van Pelt, "I have a surprise for you. Tomorrow morning I want you and your brother and sisters to come to my hotel. I want to show you something."

CHAPTER X

THE TREASURE CHEST

FREDDIE and Flossie, as well as Nan, were very much interested in Bert's new boat. The younger twins begged their brother to take them for a sail. Bert did not feel that he knew enough about handling his craft to take out passengers.

"There is something else for us to do, though," Bert announced. "Captain Van Pelt wants us to meet him at the hotel tomorrow morning."

"What for?" asked Freddie.

"He said he had a surprise."

"What kind?" inquired Flossie.

"I don't know," replied Bert, "except that he has something to show us."

The four Bobbseys could hardly wait for morning to arrive, and spent a lot of time trying to guess what the old captain intended to exhibit.

"Maybe it's something else about his daughter," suggested Nan.

"I hope it's something to eat," said Freddie.

"What shall we do this afternoon?" asked Nan.

"Well, it's blowing too hard for me to practice in my boat. Let's take a walk back in the country and see if we can find any trace of the captain's missing daughter."

"All right!" agreed Nan. "That will be a good thing to do."

At first Bert and Nan had the idea that it would be rather easy for them to make inquiries and find out something about the missing daughter, wife, and possible grandchild of Captain Van Pelt. They accordingly started out with high hopes.

"All we have to do," said Nan, "is to go around asking people if they know anybody named Debby whose father was once shipwrecked. It doesn't matter what Captain Van Pelt's daughter's married name might be, if she did marry. We know her first name is Debby."

"It wasn't really Debby," said Bert. "It was Deborah. Debby was just her nickname."

"We'll inquire for both names," said Nan. "And then maybe there's a granddaughter. We don't know what her name could be."

"We don't even know that there is a granddaughter," spoke Bert. "It might be a grandson."

The country around Storm Haven consisted of

level land, hills and valleys. Near the sea the land was quite flat. Farther back it was hilly. There were several roads leading to small villages and little towns.

"There are a lot of places around here we might go to," said Bert to his sister, as they started out. "It's hard to know which one to try first."

"I know a good way to do it," said Nan. "We'll begin at the places on our left and work toward the ones on our right."

"You mean," went on Bert, "that we'll start asking questions at the first town to the left of Storm Haven and work toward the right?"

"That's it," said Nan.

That was the way they did it. An old woman lived at the first house at which they inquired. Bert asked:

"Do you know anybody who is the lost daughter of a wrecked sea captain?"

"No, I don't want to buy any sweeping caps," she said, closing the door.

Bert and Nan looked at each other and then laughed, for they realized the speaker could not hear them.

"She's as bad as Aunt Sallie Pry," whispered Nan, referring to a nice, but deaf, old lady who sometimes came to help Mrs. Bobbsey with the housework, and who undertook to look after the twins when their parents were away.

"I guess she isn't the one we want," agreed Bert.

They went to several other houses where they made inquiries, but had no luck. At some of the places they were stared at as though people thought they were merely joking. When such was the case, Bert and his sister explained why they were asking such odd questions. As soon as they had done this, they found everybody was very eager to be of assistance.

Toward the close of the afternoon, the twins turned back toward Storm Haven, having met with no success.

"We'll try again some time," said Nan.

"Sure!" agreed Bert.

The four Bobbseys presented themselves early the following day at the hotel, and inquired for Captain Van Pelt. After good mornings were said, Flossie came right to the point.

"What are you going to show us?" she asked.

The old sailor laughed.

"You really want to know? Well, it's my treasure chest."

"Where is it?" came from Freddie.

"In my room," answered the captain. "You wait here and I'll get it. Then we'll take it down to the beach and open it."

He was gone a few minutes, and then returned carrying a wooden chest on which were many bright strips of brass. He led the way with the Bobbsey twins down to the beach not far from the hotel.

"Have you any whales' or sharks' teeth in that box?" asked Freddie, when they were all seated on the sand.

"Some teeth of sharks, yes," the captain said. "But a whale's tooth is too big for my small box."

The wind was blowing hard and the waves were quite high, even in the bay. They crashed and hissed on the sand and pebbles.

"We mustn't get too close to the water," warned Captain Van Pelt. "Let me see, now. I think I'll find some cushions of dried seaweed for you to sit on while I show you my treasure box."

He put the little chest down on the sand and walked up the beach to a place amid some rocks where there were strands of dried seaweed.

"Let me help get some!" begged Freddie.

"I want to do it, too," said Flossie.

Bert and Nan were watching a dog who was run-

ning about the sand. Suddenly the man who owned
it pointed to the water and shouted a warning.

"What's the matter?" asked Captain Van Pelt,
turning about, his arms filled with seaweed.

"A big wave is coming—look!" cried the man.
"Run back here, Jack!" he called to his dog.

Suddenly a huge billow pounded in on the shore,
flowed over the treasure box, and a moment later
washed it away before the sea captain could rescue
his property.

CHAPTER XI

THE BERRY BOY

For a second the surprise of seeing what had happened held the Bobbsey twins and Captain Van Pelt motionless on the sand. It was like seeing something happen in a dream. Then the sailor shouted:

"There goes my box! My treasure box is washed away!"

"Quick!" yelled Bert. "Maybe we can get it before it goes out too far!" In a moment he sat down and began pulling off his shoes and stockings.

"I must get it back!" cried the captain. "It has treasures in it that I was bringing back to my wife and daughter. I must save my precious box!"

Dressed as he was, and not even stopping to take off his shoes, he rushed into the water. The big wave had gone down now, but the bay was still rough because of the strong wind and the additional waves that were forming.

Freddie and Flossie had seen the carrying away

of the captain's box. For the moment they did not know what to do. Then Freddie, seeing the captain rush into the water, did the same thing himself. He did not stop to take off his shoes or stockings. Right into the water he dashed after Captain Van Pelt.

"Freddie, come back here! Let Bert try to get the box!" commanded Nan. But Freddie did not pay any attention to her cry.

By this time Bert had made himself ready to dash in without spoiling his shoes, and ran down the stretch of sand between the piles of seaweed and the edge of the water. Captain Van Pelt was already wading about, searching anxiously for his treasure box.

"I'm afraid it's gone," he said, as Bert came up beside him.

"Won't it float?" asked the Bobbsey boy.

"Not very far. It's pretty well filled up and it's bound with brass. It has a lot of heavy things in it. No, I'm afraid my box is gone."

"Maybe you can dive and get it," Freddie suggested. He had been on the public dock one day when something was knocked into the water, and had watched a sailor put on a bathing suit. By diving he had recovered the lost object.

"You can't dive in this water," said Captain Van Pelt. "It isn't deep enough for that, yet it is sufficiently so to hide my treasure box."

He and Bert continued to wade about in the place where they thought the box might be. The boy felt about with his toes, as he and some of the Storm Haven boys often did trying to find hard clams under the soft sand and mud of the bay. But he did not feel any box. Captain Van Pelt reached his hand down under the water and tried to find it, but he had no luck, either.

The wind was blowing harder and the waves were growing rougher. Seeing this, Captain Van Pelt said to Freddie:

"You had better go back to shore. The tide is coming in fast."

"Oh, I want to help find the box," the little boy said, looking toward the beach where Nan and Flossie were anxiously watching the search.

Just as Freddie turned his head, he was slapped on the back by a large wave. The little fellow was knocked down, and had Bert not been there to catch hold of him he would have been under water long enough to have choked painfully. As it was, he got soaked through. Gasping, and trying not to cry, he was carried up the sand by his brother.

"Dear me! I'm sorry about that!" said Captain Van Pelt.

"Oh, he's all right," answered Nan from shore, as she dried Freddie's face with her handkerchief and made sure he was not injured.

"Yes—I—I'm all—right!" panted the little fellow. "I'll be back in a minute and help you look for your box, Captain!"

"No, you stay there," the sailor said. "I don't believe there's any use looking further for my treasure box. It is gone forever!"

"That's too bad," Bert said.

"Yes, I'm very sorry," said the old man. "Not only did I want to show you children the treasures, but I was hoping that some day I might give them to my own daughter. She may have a little girl or boy of her own, and I was going to give some of the treasures to my grandchildren. But my chest is lost."

He began to walk back toward shore as did Bert, who said:

"Even if you should sometime get the box back again I suppose everything in it would be spoiled by the water."

"No, that's where you're mistaken," said the captain. "Not that I ever expect to find it, for the sea has it. But it was water-tight. Not a drop could get in when the lid was closed."

"Well, that was lucky," said Bert.

"Yes, but it doesn't do me any good," sighed Captain Van Pelt. "I spent a lot of time and labor making that box water-tight to hold my treasures, and then the sea comes up and takes it from me. Well, it's just another loss—first my wife and daughter, and now my box."

He seemed sadder than usual, and Bert wished that he and Nan might do something to cheer him up. Nan spoke again of the chance of finding some trace of the missing daughter by inquiring for her in the neighborhood.

"I don't know why it is," he said to the children, "but somehow I have a feeling that if my daughter and whatever family she may have are alive, I'll find them around Storm Haven. That's why I always seem to come back here. I've no other reason for anchoring at this place except that I hope to locate my people some day."

"We'll help you all we can," promised Nan.

Several times during the next few days Captain Van Pelt gave Bert additional sailing lessons which were slowly making a young sailor out of the lad. Once or twice he had taken the cat boat out alone while the captain watched from the dock. Bert did very well.

Then one day the old sailor told Bert that he had to go away.

"I've had word from your father," he said. "He wants me to get him another load of lumber. But I'll be back!"

"Do you think it would be all right for me to take my boat out alone?" asked Bert.

"Better not, my boy," replied Captain Van Pelt. "While I'm gone I'll have a friend of mine, Bill Radder, give you a few pointers about sailing. Bill is an old sailor. He keeps a little shop for seamen just off the public dock."

"I know the place," Bert said.

"Sure I'll give him lessons!" declared Mr. Radder when Captain Van Pelt introduced Bert. "Glad to! The more a boy knows about sailing a boat the better off he is. Come and tell me any time you want a lesson, Bert, and we'll go out together."

As a sort of farewell party the Bobbsey twins went aboard the *Debby D* before she sailed for Georgia. As they were leaving the public dock to be rowed out to the ship by Pegleg Baldwin, the children saw Miss Perkin.

"Let's ask her to come with us," suggested Nan to Bert.

The former stowaway, still wearing her trousers and coat, was very glad to be with the twins.

"I want to hear the parrot talk again, too," she said.

"And don't you want to see some more bambooing on Mr. Pegleg?" asked Flossie.

"Tattooing! Tattooing!" corrected Bert, laughing.

"He has a dog on his leg," said Freddie. "And I don't mean on his wooden leg, either."

Aboard the *Debby D* Captain Van Pelt made his visitors welcome, while Mr. Green talked, laughed, whistled, and even tried to sing.

"Well, I'll see you when I get back," the captain called to the Bobbsey twins and Miss Perkin, as Pegleg Baldwin was leaving to row them back to shore. "Have you a job yet?" he asked the stowaway.

"Not yet," she answered. "And I certainly need one."

Nan and Bert wished they might help her find one. They were talking about it one afternoon a few days later, when they had come in from bathing and were resting on the side porch of Button-

ball Cottage. Mrs. Bobbsey was lying down upstairs and Freddie and Flossie were playing out on
the street.

Just then a knock sounded at the back door.
Dinah went to see who it was, and presently came
out to Nan and Bert and said:

"Ah doan't want t' bodder yo' ma, fo' she's lyin'
down. But de berry boy am heah."

"Who?" asked Nan.

"De berry boy," repeated Dinah, "wif a funny
animule."

"We don't know anybody named Berry," Bert
said. "We'd better go see who it is, Nan."

CHAPTER XII

THE SWAMP BEAR

NAN BOBBSEY came back to the porch where Bert was still reading. She was smiling.

"Who was it?" asked her brother.

"It was a berry boy all right," Nan answered. "He was selling huckleberries, and I'd like to get some, for Dinah says they'll be good in a pie."

"So the boy sells berries even if his name isn't Berry," remarked Bert. "Well, you have my permission to get the berries, Nan."

"I need some change," she said. "Perhaps you have some, Bert. I don't want to bother Mother for she is resting. I'll buy the berries if you let me have the money. Have you any?"

"Oh, yes, I have some," said Bert, jingling a new coin purse which his father had given him on his latest visit. "But if I'm going to spend money for berries I want to see that they're good."

"A lot you know about berries!" laughed Nan.

"Well, I know a lot about huckleberry pie!"

chuckled Bert. "So I'll take a look. We won't have to bother Mother."

Nan accompanied her brother to the back steps where Dinah had left the boy. He proved to be a brown-skinned country lad with a smiling face and dark eyes. On the steps he had set down a tin pail containing about two quarts of huckleberries.

"These are fresh," he said, seeing Bert. "I picked them myself. They're all I have left so I'll let you have them for ten cents a quart. Generally I get twelve, but these are the last two quarts."

"Where did you sell the others?" asked Bert.

"Up at the hotel. I sold eight quarts there. That was all they wanted today. Usually they take more. But this is the middle of the week. They have more guests over the week-end so they buy more berries."

"Will two quarts be enough for a pie, Nan?" asked Bert.

"Of course!" she answered.

"Then we'll take these," went on Bert. "Where'd you pick 'em?"

"On the edge of the swamp back of Railford," answered the berry boy. "That's about three miles from here."

"Are there any more huckleberries there?"

"Heaps of 'em this time of year," said the boy. "I can sell all I pick and more."

Nan wondered why Bert was asking so many questions, but she did not like to inquire why just then. Dinah brought out a dish into which the boy emptied the berries, and Bert asked him his name.

"Ed Bolby," the boy answered. "I live in Railford. Much obliged for buying these," he said.

"You're welcome," answered Bert. "Do you think I could pick any huckleberries if I went to that swamp?" he asked.

"Sure," replied Ed Bolby. "There're heaps of 'em. You could sell 'em, too."

"That's a good thing to know," said Bert. Nan wondered what plan her brother had in mind. A moment later she forgot all about huckleberries, for she saw a strange little furry animal walk out from beneath a rosebush toward the berry boy, who stood on the bottom step ready to leave.

"Oh, Bert! It's a skunk!" cried Nan, getting ready to bolt into the house.

"Where?" asked Bert.

"There!" cried Nan, pointing.

The berry boy laughed, then said:

"That isn't a skunk. It's my tame raccoon. I often take him with me when I come to sell berries. Folks at the hotel like to see him do tricks and they sometimes pay me for having him perform. Here, Soapy!" he called.

The black-faced raccoon with rings of fur on his bushy tail, and paws that were almost like little hands, came scampering toward his master.

"Up!" called Ed, and the raccoon climbed up the boy's side and perched on his shoulder.

"Oh, how cute!" exclaimed Nan, no longer afraid.

"What did you say his name was?" asked Bert.

"I call him Soapy. You see, raccoons wash nearly everything they eat in water before they'll nibble it. Since he washes himself so often I call my raccoon 'Soapy'."

"It's a good name," agreed Bert. "What tricks can he do?"

"He turns somersaults, stands on his hind legs, and plays dead," Ed answered. "Here, I'll show you. But not for money," he quickly added. "You're customers of mine now, same as the hotel is, and I'll have Soapy do tricks for you for nothing. Down, Soapy!" he ordered, and the cute little animal scrambled to the porch.

"Stand up!" Ed ordered, and Soapy stood on his hind paws like a little dog.

"Over you go!" was the next order, and Soapy turned three somersaults, one right after the other.

"Oh, I think he's just lovely!" murmured Nan. "Here come Freddie and Flossie!" she said. "Let them see!"

The smaller Bobbsey twins, who had been playing down the street, were as much interested in the raccoon as Bert and Nan had been. They watched him do the first two tricks again, and then Ed ordered:

"Play dead!"

At once Soapy stretched out, and looked as if he had no life in him. But he was as lively as a cricket a moment later when his master called:

"Time to eat!"

Up he jumped and looked about him.

"Oh, it's too bad to fool him," said Bert. "Will he eat something if I get it?"

"Yes," Ed answered.

"And will he wash it in water?" asked Nan.

"I guess he will," said the berry boy.

"What does he like best to eat?" Bert inquired.

"He's very fond of green corn," said Ed. "Perhaps you have part of an ear you can spare."

"There's some corn in the kitchen!" exclaimed Nan. "Dinah is husking it to boil. I'll get part of an ear, and break off a nice piece for your animal."

"Let me feed it to him!" begged Flossie.

"No, I want to!" cried Freddie.

"I think we had better let Ed do it," suggested Bert. "He knows his pet raccoon better than we do. Soapy might not like to take corn from strangers."

"Oh, Soapy isn't fussy," laughed the berry boy. "He'll make friends with anybody. Here, let him sit on your shoulder," he said. Before Freddie could object, Ed had placed the tame raccoon on his shoulder, where the cute little pet cuddled down, putting his cold nose on the little boy's neck.

"Oh!" exclaimed Freddie. "He tickles me!"

"Let him tickle me!" begged Flossie.

So, while waiting for Nan to come back with the ear of corn, the berry boy perched Soapy on Flossie's shoulder where the little black nose tickled her neck too, much to her delight.

Nan came out with part of an ear of corn and Dinah followed to the kitchen door.

"Whut all is gwine on out yeah?" asked the fat cook.

"It's the berry boy's pet raccoon," Bert explained.

"Ha! I seen lots ob dem down Souf where I

comes from!" chuckled Dinah. "Dey won't hurt yo'!"

Besides the corn, Nan brought out a little basin of water which she set down on the steps. When Ed had handed his raccoon the ear, the little animal took it in his paws, which were like baby hands, dipped it in the basin of water, and then began to nibble at it.

"Oh, isn't he cute!" exclaimed Nan.

"Where did you get him?" asked Bert.

"In the woods near the swamp," Ed replied. "He was a little baby 'coon when I found him. Somebody had shot his mother, I guess, for Soapy was all alone. I took him home with the berries I picked and I've had him ever since."

The Bobbsey twins were delighted to watch the pet, and when Ed had to leave, Freddie wanted Bert to promise to go look for another raccoon some day.

"Maybe I will," Bert said.

A little later, when Freddie and Flossie had gone to sail the toy boat in the hotel lagoon, and Dinah was making the huckleberry pie, Nan said to Bert:

"Did you mean what you told Freddie about getting him a raccoon?"

"I'm not sure that I can get him one,' Bert said, "but I'm going to that swamp and pick huckleberries in a couple of days."

"You are?" exclaimed Nan. "Why, do you want more pie?"

"Yes. Also, I want to pick berries and sell them around Storm Haven and get some money."

"What do you want the money for?" asked his sister.

"To buy seat cushions for my cat boat," was Bert's answer. "Will you come to pick huckleberries with me?"

"Why, yes, I will," Nan promised. "And I'll help you sell them, too!"

"Good!" cried Bert. "Then I'll give you a ride in my boat when I know how to sail her better."

It was a few days after that, when Mrs. Bobbsey went off in the automobile to visit some friends, that Bert decided to go to the swamp after huckleberries. His mother gave him and Nan permission to go. Freddie and Flossie teased so hard to accompany them so they might look for a raccoon that they, also, were taken along.

"Don't you think the walk will be too far?"

"No!" they answered in a chorus.

"We want to find a raccoon!" added Freddie.

So, taking pails and baskets to hold the fruit, and also a little lunch to eat when they might feel hungry, the Bobbsey twins started for the swamp. Ed Bolby had told them how to get there.

Though Freddie and Flossie were smaller than Nan and Bert, they made no complaint as they trudged the two or more miles to the berrying place. It was a good road and the day was not too hot.

They reached the patch of woods spoken of by the raccoon boy, as Freddie sometimes called him, and soon were within sight of a swampy bit of ground covered thickly with huckleberry bushes. They were so high in many places that they were above the heads of all the twins.

"We can keep on the paths," suggested Nan. "Then we won't get lost."

There were several trails through the huckleberry swamp, which was often visited in the berry season. On either side of the paths there were dense undergrowths of briars, bushes, tall ferns, and a tangle of weeds.

"Oh, look at the berries!" suddenly exclaimed Nan, as she saw clusters of the blue fruit on a bush.

"Don't you see any raccoons?" asked Flossie.

"We came after berries," said Bert. "We aren't going to pick raccoons."

"Well, Freddie and I want a tame raccoon that washes the things it eats," said Flossie.

The children began picking the berries, which were plentiful. It cannot be said that Flossie and Freddie picked a great number. Now and then the small twins would stop and walk along the path, peering into the bushes for a sight of a raccoon, but they were disappointed each time.

However, when Bert and Nan had their baskets nearly half filled, Flossie and Freddie came running back from one of their little jaunts. Their eyes were wide open in excitement.

"We've found him!" shouted Flossie.

"He's right back there!" added Freddie, pointing in the direction from which they had come.

"What is?" asked Nan.

"The raccoon," said Freddie. "We saw his black nose, and he's standing on his hind legs and eating huckleberries."

"He's a big one, too!" said Flossie.

"Let's go see!" proposed Nan to Bert.

"You bet," agreed Bert.

The older twins followed the younger pair along the swamp path. Suddenly Freddie, who was ahead, came to a stop. He pointed toward some waving bushes and said:

"There's the raccoon!"

A moment later Bert and Nan had a glimpse of the animal. No sooner had they seen him than Nan gave a scream and cried:

"That isn't a raccoon! It's a bear!"

CHAPTER XIII

LOST

For a moment Bert Bobbsey thought his sister Nan was mistaken in thinking she had seen a bear in the huckleberry bushes. But when Bert took a second look he was sure she was right.

There was no doubt about it. Standing up on his hind legs, not far from the Bobbsey twins, but separated from them by a screen of bushes almost as high as the animal's head, was a brown, shaggy bear. His fur was so dark that it looked almost black.

"Say, he's a big one!" spoke Freddie, not taking care to lower his voice.

"Hush! Hush!" begged Nan in a frantic whisper. "Don't let him hear you!"

"Why not?" asked Flossie, speaking as loudly as Freddie had. "He looks like a nice bear. Maybe he's tame and can do tricks."

"Oh, will you hush!" commanded Nan.

Her voice sounded so stern that without knowing why they did it, the smaller twins cowered down behind some shrubbery where they had been picking berries. In this position they could not see the bear's head over the tops of the bushes from which he was pulling the blue fruit.

"I wonder if he can see us?" murmured Flossie in Freddie's ear.

"I don't believe he can," answered the little boy. "But isn't it fun to find a bear the first time we come to the berry swamp?"

"Lots of fun," Flossie agreed.

"Will you be quiet!" cautioned Nan. "You'll have that bear chasing us in another minute if you keep on talking." She was whispering, and when she had finished this low-voiced warning to the small twins she seemed very much worried.

"What shall we do?" she asked Bert quietly.

"We'd better get away from here," was his answer. "It may be a tame bear, as Flossie says, but even a tame one doesn't like to be bothered when he's eating. So let's sneak away quietly."

"Yes," agreed Nan, still speaking in a whisper, and glancing down, first at Flossie and Freddie cuddled at her feet, then across the tops of the bushes at the bear. "Now don't make a noise," she cautioned them. "We're going to leave this place."

"Shall we take our berry baskets with us?" asked Freddie, remembering to lower his voice this time.

"Yes," Bert answered, "we'll take all our berries. No use leaving them for the bear. He can pick his own—the bushes are filled with them."

During this little talk the animal had not stirred from where he was standing amid the shrubs. He was very busy eating. He stood upright on his hind legs as do most bears when they are feeding from bushes, or when they are doing tricks. Because he stood on his hind legs Flossie thought he might be a trick animal.

"Oh, look at him! Isn't he cute?" cried Flossie. "Let's take him home for a pet."

"Don't be too sure you want such a pet," said Nan. "The bear has real sharp teeth."

"Then I guess I don't," said Flossie, realizing the danger.

The way in which the bear ate the huckleberries was very funny. It would stretch out one big, shaggy paw with its long, curved claws, and pull toward its open mouth a branch of a bush which had on it many ripe berries. When it was almost between the bear's teeth, the animal would move its paw along it. The curved claws would strip off the berries and the foot part of the paw would thrust them into the open mouth almost as if a broom had swept them there.

In spite of the danger present, Nan and Bert could not help standing there a moment looking at the clever way in which the bear fed himself. After swallowing the berries which it had put into its mouth with the left paw, the bear would use its right paw and do the same thing. Of course, by thus stripping the branch the animal got plenty of small twigs. But it did not seem to object to them, eating them together with the berries.

"That bear certainly is having a good feed," whispered Bert.

"Yes, indeed," added Nan. "But let's get away from here!"

She started to move back, reaching down to take hold of Flossie's hand.

"You take Freddie," she told Bert, while the older Bobbsey boy guided his brother.

Then, just as the children started to hurry away, carrying the pails and baskets half-filled with huckleberries, the bear either smelled them, saw them, or heard them. The Bobbsey twins could not be sure which it was. At any rate, the animal stopped eating, looked in the direction of the children, and then lunged through the bushes as if coming at them.

"Oh, he'll get us!" screamed Nan. "Run! Run!"

"Don't let him get me if he isn't a tame bear!" begged Flossie.

"If I could find a club," exclaimed Bert, "I'd bang him on the nose. That's the place to hit a bear."

"Don't you dare stop to hit this bear with a club, Bert Bobbsey!" ordered Nan. "You run along and take Freddie with you. I'll look after Flossie. Oh, this is terrible."

"Maybe you could hit him with a stone," suggested Freddie, running his fastest and keeping a firm hold of Bert's hand. Bert let Flossie and Nan get ahead of him and Freddie. It was Bert's idea to protect his two sisters if the bear should come too close.

Behind the children could be heard the crashing and crackling of the high bushes as the animal tore its way through them.

"Oh, he's coming after us!" cried Nan.

"Maybe he can't find us," suggested Bert. "The bushes are pretty high."

"Bears can smell you," Freddie stated, as he stumbled along beside Bert. The little fellow was going so fast that some of the huckleberries spilled out from his basket. But he did not care about that. The thing to do was to get away from the bear.

It did not take much of this fast running to cause Flossie and Freddie to get out of breath. Bert and Nan also felt the strain, and when Flossie whimpered that she could not run any more Nan was forced to slacken her pace.

"But you must run, Flossie!" Nan said.

"I can't!" wailed the little girl. "My legs hurt!"

"So do mine!" said Freddie.

"Hark!' whispered Bert, who had come to a stop with his small brother. "Listen!"

They all stopped instantly.

"What is it?" whispered Nan.

"Do you hear that bear coming after us now?" asked Bert.

Nan listened intently.

"No," she answered, "I can't hear him."

"I think perhaps he's lost track of us," replied her brother.

"Oh, I hope he has!" murmured Nan. "If he'll only run the other way everything will be all right."

They stood where they were for several seconds. It was so still that Nan was sure she could hear the thumping and beating of her own heart. But they did not hear the crackle of bushes which would indicate that the bear was crashing his way toward them. There was no sound at all.

Suddenly, from far off in the distance, there could be heard the barking of a dog. Catching the sound, Nan and Bert looked at each other. Then Bert said, speaking louder this time:

"I guess some dog got on the trail of the bear and is chasing him. That's why the animal isn't following us. He's running away from the dog and in the opposite direction from where we are."

"I'm glad!" exclaimed Nan.

"Is the dog hunting the bear?" asked Freddie.

"Well, you might call it that," admitted Bert.

"Maybe men with guns are hunting the bear, too," said Flossie. "Hunters take dogs with them, don't they?"

"Yes," said Bert. "But this isn't the hunting season. Anyhow, some dog got after our bear and chased him away."

"Don't call him our bear," said Nan with a little laugh. "I don't want any bears."

"I'd like a bear if he was a tame one," said Freddie.

"So would I," chimed in Flossie.

"Don't be silly!" chided Nan. "Oh, but I'm so glad that bear isn't chasing us any more," she added. "Do you think we'd better go back home, Bert?"

"No," answered the older Bobbsey boy after thinking the matter over. "There's no use wasting this chance to get a lot of berries. Look how thick they grow around here, Nan."

"Yes, there are lots of 'em," Nan agreed, glancing at the bushes amid which they now stood. "We could soon fill our pails and baskets here."

"Then let's do it," suggested Bert. "I'll get enough to sell at the hotel and around the village, and then I can get those cushions for my sailboat."

"I'll give you all the berries I pick," promised Nan. "Those Freddie and Flossie have will be enough for Dinah to make us huckleberry pie."

"Thanks," answered Bert. "I'll take you for a ride in my boat as soon as Captain Van Pelt comes back and gives me a few more lessons."

"Are you sure he's coming back?" asked Nan.

"Oh, yes. He told me he would. The last thing he said was that he had a new idea about looking for his daughter around here."

"I hope he finds her," murmured Nan.

"So do I," said Bert. "But it would be swell if we could solve the mystery for him."

"Wouldn't it!" agreed Nan. "Well, let's pick the berries and get through with it. I'm sort of nervous staying in this swamp where there's a bear loose."

"Oh, I don't believe he'll come back this way," was Bert's opinion. "That dog probably chased him a long way off."

"Won't we ever see him again?" asked Flossie.

"I hope not!" laughed Nan.

"Well, I'd like to see him," remarked Freddie.

"Come on, now, pick your berries!" suggested Nan, and all the twins were soon busy. Now and then they stopped to listen, but heard no alarming sounds. The bear seemed far enough away.

The berries were so thick on the bushes in this part of the swamp that the children were not long in filling their baskets and pails. Flossie and Freddie each had a basket, as they were lighter for their small hands to carry. Bert and Nan had large pails which, when filled with berries, would be rather heavy.

Though the place where the huckleberries grew in such profusion was called a swamp, it was only in the lowest place that there was anything like a bog. Where the twins were picking huckleberries it was fairly high and dry ground, but thick with bushes and small trees. Paths crossed the berry swamp in several directions.

"Well, my pail's full!" Bert finally announced.

"Mine is nearly," added Nan. "How about you children?" she asked Flossie and Freddie.

"My berries are nearly to the top," said the little boy. "But I stopped picking to eat a few."

"So did I," confessed Flossie. Neither she nor Freddie needed to say this. One look at their faces showed they had been munching berries.

"Well, don't eat too many," warned Nan. "Remember that we have a little picnic lunch to eat, and it's about time we did that, now that we have all the berries we can carry."

In a short time the baskets of the small twins were filled. Then, finding a little clearing in the bushes where an old log could be used for seats, the children sat down and began to eat the delicious lunch Dinah had put up for them. It was about noon, Bert decided, after looking at the sun which was almost directly overhead.

They rested a little while after their meal. Then, as Bert was eager to get back to Storm Haven and sell his berries that afternoon, he suggested that they return. They started along what they thought was the right path and continued for some little time.

Suddenly Bert stopped, and said:

"Wait a minute."

"What's the matter?" asked Nan nervously. "Do you hear that bear again?"

"No," Bert answered, "but I think we're going the wrong way."

"The wrong way!" exclaimed Nan.

"Yes. I don't remember coming along this path, do you?"

Nan did not, and said so. She looked about her, but could see no familiar landmarks. She had noticed several large rocks when she had entered the swamp. None of these could be seen now.

"I guess we'd better go back a ways and take another path," Bert said. "This isn't the right one."

"I'll tell you what made us come the wrong way," said Nan.

"What?"

"Running away from that bear."

"I guess that was it," agreed Bert. "Anyhow, we'll soon be on the right path."

They went back and reached a place where three paths met. Then, after looking about him, Bert decided on the middle one. They had not traveled this course very far before the older Bobbsey boy stopped again.

"What's the matter now?" asked Nan.

"I—I guess we're lost," Bert said. "I mean, we're in the same berry swamp we were when we started. But there are so many paths I don't know which one to take to get back home."

"Oh!" gasped Nan. "What are we going to do?"

CHAPTER XIV

THE WRONG PATH

FLOSSIE and Freddie did not appear to be at all alarmed at what Bert had said about being lost. In fact, it is doubtful if the small twins had heard him, for just at that moment Freddie and his small sister had seen a little animal with bright eyes peering out at them from beneath a clump of grass.

"Maybe it's a baby bear," Flossie suggested, her voice showing how delighted she would be if it were.

"I think it's a raccoon," suggested Freddie.

"Never mind about little bears or raccoons," broke in Nan. "The point is, how are we going to get home?"

"We'll walk," Freddie said promptly.

"But we don't know the way," Nan objected. "Bert says we're lost."

"Are we?" asked Flossie, looking at her big brother.

"I'm afraid we are," Bert was forced to admit.

He had been looking around since they had come to this second stop, but was not sure if he should keep on, or go back to the place where the three paths joined, and try the left one or the right one. Taking the middle one had steered them entirely wrong.

"Oh, dear!" sighed Nan. Then, noting the worried look on the faces of Freddie and Flossie, she knew she would have to keep up their courage as well as her own. She laughed a little, though she did not feel much like it, and said:

"I guess we won't be lost very long. Bert and I will find the way home somehow."

"Sure!" Bert added. "But there's no use keeping on in this direction. We may only get deeper in the swamp."

"Shall we turn back?" asked Nan.

"It's the only thing we can do. When we get to the place where the three paths meet we can wait a while."

"What for?" Nan wanted to know.

"So the sun will begin to go down a bit," Bert replied. "You see," he continued, "when we came in the berry swamp this morning the sun was at our backs. That meant we were walking toward the West. To go home again we should have the sun at our backs and walk East. Now that it's about noon and the sun is right overhead, I can't tell East from West."

"Well, if you think you can find your way after we get back to the three paths and wait for the sun to begin to go down so we'll know which is the West, I suppose it's the best thing to do," said Nan.

"Sure," said Bert. "Come on, Flossie and Freddie!" he called.

The younger twins had wandered off a little way down the path by themselves but were not out of sight. They had set down their baskets of berries carefully so as to spill none of them.

"What are you after?" called Bert to them.

"That little bear I saw," Flossie answered.

" 'Tisn't a bear, it's a raccoon," insisted Freddie.

"Better not go any farther," warned Bert. "I don't believe it's a raccoon, and it certainly isn't a little bear."

"It's something!" Freddie said. "Look!"

He pointed beneath another clump of grass. The animal with the bright eyes had scampered from beneath the first one, and now, as if playing hide-and-seek, was looking out from another.

"What is it, Bert?" asked Nan.

"If you ask me, I think it's a muskrat," Bert answered.

"Oh, a rat!" cried Nan.

"There's nothing to be afraid of," said Bert. "Muskrats aren't like regular rats. Of course, they might bite you the same way a kitten would scratch you if you grabbed its tail. But I don't believe Flossie and Freddie can get near enough to this muskrat to be in any danger. Look! There he goes!"

While Bert was talking, the small twins were edging closer and closer to the clump of grass concealing the muskrat. As Bert finished speaking, the little animal made a dart, scampered over an open place and plunged, with a splash, into a pool of water.

"There he goes!" shouted Flossie.

"Look at him swim!" yelled Freddie.

Fascinated, they stood watching the creature, which was soon out of sight.

"Well, we certainly are having plenty of menagerie excitement today," said Nan with a laugh. "First a bear, then a muskrat, and——"

"Perhaps we'll find a raccoon before we get home," broke in Freddie.

"Maybe we'll run into a whole circus," said Bert

in a low voice to Nan, as the small twins went to pick up their baskets of berries.

"What do you mean?" asked Nan.

"Well, it may be quite a long time before we get back home," was Bert's answer.

"Oh," murmured Nan, "don't you think you can find the way after we get to the paths?"

"I'll see," was all Bert would answer.

It wasn't very difficult to retrace their steps back to the place where the three paths came together.

"We'll mark this middle one that we just took, which was the wrong one, with some of these white stones," suggested Bert, picking up a few pebbles and making a little pile out of them. "Then, if we have to come back here again, we'll know which path we used."

"Are you going to take the right-hand path or the left-hand one?" asked Nan.

"What do you think?" Bert wanted to know.

"Well, it always sounds better to say you took the right path even if it turns out to be the wrong one," Nan remarked with a little laugh. "I mean, when you're lost, I think it's better to take the right-hand path instead of the left-hand one."

"Unless you happen to be left-handed," agreed Bert. also laughing. Neither he nor Nan wanted to get the small twins frightened over being lost. "All right," Bert went on, "we'll go to the right."

This they did, starting to walk into the berry patch this new way. The huckleberry bushes were still thick about them, and the dark, bluish-gray fruit gleamed in the sun. Nan was glad it was a sunshiny day. It did not seem quite so miserable to be lost in the sunshine as it did in the rain. Still, it was not any fun to be lost at all.

On and on walked the Bobbsey twins. Bert was almost wishing, now, that he and the others had not gathered so many berries. The loads were heavy to carry, especially for the small twins.

More than once the baskets Freddie and Flossie were carrying had bumped against their legs and the small trees and bushes along the path, so that some of the berries had scattered out. Neither Nan nor Bert chided their little brother and sister about this. It was bad enough to be tired and discouraged and lost without having to stop and pick up dropped berries.

The twins, with Bert in the lead and Nan bringing up the rear, had walked perhaps half a mile down the right-hand path, when Bert again came to a stop.

"What is it now?" asked Nan wearily. She looked

about her for a place to sit down but saw none. There was boggy and marshy ground with big hummocks of grass on each side of the path of hard dirt.

"This doesn't seem to be the right way," Bert said. "I can tell by the sun, which is going down a little in the West, that we're headed in the wrong direction."

"What shall we do?" Nan asked.

"Go back to the three paths and this time take the left one," said her brother.

"Oh, I'm sorry I suggested taking the right path this time," Nan said, trying to smile, but not succeeding very well. "This is the time when the right path was the wrong one."

"You couldn't help it," said Bert. "Never mind, I think we'll hit the right way now."

Wearily they trudged back to the junction of the three paths. This time, after letting Freddie and Flossie rest a while, they took the left path. It was the only one remaining for them to travel.

"I'm sure we're right now," Bert said.

When they had gone about three quarters of a mile, Bert again stopped and shook his head.

"This doesn't seem right," he said.

"Oh, dear!" gasped Nan. Tears came into her

eyes. She was so tired, and she knew Flossie and Freddie must be weary also.

"This is hard luck!" said Bert.

"What are we going to do?" asked Nan.

Just then they heard the breaking of bushes and the swishing of leaves.

"Somebody's coming this way," said Nan in a low voice.

Bert listened and agreed with her.

"Oh, maybe it's the bear coming back!" exclaimed Freddie who, with his small sister, had put down his basket of berries and was sitting on a flat stone.

"Nonsense! It isn't the bear!" declared Bert.

"Then maybe it's my muskrat," said Freddie.

"I hope it's a little raccoon," suggested Flossie. "I'd like a raccoon like that boy had."

The sound of breaking bushes and swishing leaves became louder. Then the barking of a dog could be heard.

Nan and Bert looked at each other. A dog had barked before, after they had run away from the bear.

With anxious eyes the Bobbsey twins looked in the direction of the sound. The noise was coming nearer.

"More trouble," gasped Nan.

Bert put his finger to his lips.

"Sh!" he said, looking toward Freddie and Flossie. who were wide-eyed.

Nan nodded, although she was in a panic.

CHAPTER XV

OLD CHURCH

SUDDENLY through the bushes at the side of the path a dog made its appearance. It was a friendly black and white animal which wagged its tail when it saw the Bobbsey children.

In another moment a nice old man appeared. At least, that was what Flossie called him afterward —a nice old man.

"Hello, children!" he said. He was rather ragged looking, with long white hair and a white beard. "Are you lost?"

Bert had not minded admitting to his sister Nan that he was lost. But when a stranger, even though he was a nice old man, asked that question, Bert was not quite so ready to acknowledge that he had mistaken the way. So, instead of saying, right off. that he did not know how to get back to Button-ball Cottage, he replied:

"Thank you, but I guess maybe we can find our way after a while, sir."

"Can you? That's good," said the old man with a pleasant smile. "I thought perhaps you were lost."

"Oh, we are!" exclaimed Nan, having no consideration for Bert's pride or feelings. "We are lost! We've been wandering around for an hour or more and don't know which way to go."

"I could find the right path if I had a little more time," mumbled Bert.

"Where do you want to go?" asked the old man.

"Back to Storm Haven," Nan replied.

Flossie also said something in a whisper to Freddie. The old man saw her. Smiling, he inquired:

"What did you say, my little golden-haired girl?"

Flossie blushed, looked down, scraped one toe in the dirt of the path, but did not answer.

"She said," volunteered Freddie, "that you looked like some of the pictures of Santa Claus."

"Oh, what a funny thing to say!" gasped Nan.

"Thank you!" laughed the nice old man. "Well, to tell you the truth, I have hair and beard like some Santa Claus pictures, I believe. As a matter of fact, an artist once had me pose for him so he could make a painting of St. Nicholas. But I'm not Santa Claus by any means. I'm just a muskrat-hunter and live in my cottage about half a mile from here on the edge of the woods. So if you are really lost I'll be glad to show you the way back to Storm Haven. You're headed in the wrong direction."

"Are we?" asked Bert, willing now to admit that he was wrong. "Then I guess we are lost, sir."

"As if there was any doubt about it!" murmured Nan.

"Do you really hunt muskrats?" asked Flossie. She and her small brother were much interested in the nice old man now.

"Yes, I really do," he answered. "Most folks around here know me. I'm Sim Rollin, and I've lived here in the woods near the swamp many years. I make my living by trapping and shooting muskrats in the winter. In summer I sell fruits, flowers and berries."

"What do you do with the muskrats you get?" asked Freddie.

"Sell them so men can make coats out of the fur," was the answer.

"My mother has a muskrat fur coat!" exclaimed Flossie. "Did you catch the skins for her?"

"That would be hard to say," answered Mr. Rollin. "I hardly think so."

"We saw a muskrat a little while ago," went on Freddie. "Do you want to catch him?"

"No," answered the hunter. "The fur of muskrats isn't good until winter comes. Then it is fine and thick and glossy. I see you came here to get berries," he went on, looking at the pails and baskets. "You had good luck and then you got lost. I guess you went too deep in the swamp for berries. There is no need to do that. Plenty grow on the high and dry edges."

"No, we didn't exactly go too far in," Bert answered. "We saw a bear and we ran away in such a hurry I didn't notice which way we went, and when I tried to get back on the right path I couldn't."

"A bear, eh?" exclaimed Mr. Rollin. "There haven't been any in these woods or swamps for several years. They must be coming back. I'll have to get my gun ready this fall."

"Was he a tame bear?" asked Freddie.

"No, I don't believe so," was the answer. "There used to be a number of wild bears in this region. Then they disappeared. But they may be coming back."

"Are they dangerous?" asked Bert.

"Not especially so," said Mr. Rollin. "A bear will nearly always run away from you. It's only if you bother him while he is eating or if he thinks you are going to corner him that he will come at you."

"I guess this one didn't like to have us watch him eat berries," said Nan.

"Very likely," agreed Mr. Rollin. "You were in no great danger."

"And after we ran away," added Nan, "we heard a dog barking. We thought maybe it was chasing the bear."

"It was probably my dog," admitted the musk-rat-hunter. "I heard him barking a little while ago but didn't pay any attention to him. Then he came running back to my cabin. I suppose you children are tired after tramping about, and would like to get home."

"Indeed we would, thank you," spoke Nan.

"Well, if you'll come with me to my shack I'll harness my horse and take you to Storm Haven. I have a pony and cart that I use to go to and from the village when I have something to sell," he added. "I haven't anything just now, but I'll take you in just the same."

"I'd like to have a ride," said Flossie.

"So would I," agreed Freddie.

It was not far to the shack of the kind muskrat-hunter. A little later, seated in the cart, the Bobbsey twins were on their way back to Storm Haven. The fat pony jogged along slowly through the woods and the dry part of the swamp. Mr. Rollin showed Bert how he had made a wrong turn and blundered away from town instead of toward it.

"But I don't blame you for getting lost,'" said the hunter. "The bushes are so high and thick at this time of year that unless you know this region pretty well it's impossible to tell which way to go."

Now that she was no longer worried about being lost, Nan had a chance to turn her thoughts in another direction. She was thinking of Captain Van Pelt and his missing wife and daughter. As she never let a chance slip by, she decided to ask Mr. Rollin if he knew anything about the mystery.

"Hm, so the old sea captain came back to find his wife and little girl missing, did he?" commented the muskrat-hunter when Bert and Nan, in turn, had told the story.

"Yes," Nan answered, "and he sort of thinks his daughter might be living around here. He isn't sure, though."

"And he doesn't know her name?" asked the hunter.

"Not if she married," Bert said. "He thinks

maybe she did, and may have a little girl or boy.

"Do you know any such people?" asked Nan.

"No, I'm sorry to say I don't," answered Mr. Rollin. "Of course, the vicinity of Storm Haven is a good place in which to look for seafaring folks, but I don't know any lady or little child who might be seeking a lost father and grandfather. If we only knew their names, it would help."

"That's what makes it so hard," said Bert.

Suddenly Mr. Rollin appeared to have an idea. His eyes brightened. Looking at Nan and Bert, he asked:

"Did you ever inquire at Old Church?"

"What old church?" asked Bert.

"What! Don't you know about Old Church back in the country about five miles, where George Washington is said to have worshiped once with some of his officers?" asked Mr. Rollin.

"No, we don't know that church," Bert answered, wondering what it could have to do with the missing relatives of Captain Van Pelt.

"Then I must tell you about it!" said the muskrat-hunter.

CHAPTER XVI

THE NAME DEBBY

SIM ROLLIN was urging his pony along the road. The Bobbsey twins were having a nice ride and were in no particular hurry to get back home, except that Bert was thinking about his huckleberries.

"If I don't sell them today, I can do so tomorrow," he said. "So we'll have time, Mr. Rollin, to hear about Old Church."

"If you like, I can show it to you," went on the muskrat-hunter. "It isn't far out of our way if we go by this road, and you say you aren't in a hurry."

"No, we aren't," spoke Nan. "Mother doesn't expect us home until late afternoon, and we had our lunch while we were in the swamp."

"Then I'll drive you to Old Church, as we call it," said Mr. Rollin. "That's the place for you to try to find out something about Captain Van Pelt's missing folks."

The twins were eager to continue their search.

"Would the minister at the church know?" asked Nan.

"It isn't likely," answered the hunter. "He has not been there more than a couple of years. You said Captain Van Pelt's wife and daughter mysteriously vanished a long time ago."

"Yes," Bert answered. "He doesn't know just when they went away."

"I see," said Mr. Rollin. "Yet, since his folks were seafaring people, it is possible that they live somewhere near the ocean. This Old Church is as good a place as any to inquire about them."

"If the minister hasn't been there very long how is he going to know?" asked Bert, who was rather puzzled as was also Nan.

The younger twins did not take much interest in the captain's mystery. They had seen a bear, they had gathered berries, and were now having a ride. That was enough for them.

"If the minister doesn't know, and 'tisn't likely he would," said the muskrat-hunter, "you might be able to tell by the book."

"The book!" exclaimed Nan.

"Yes," was the answer. "You see, this church is very old Folks come from all over to look at it. They go inside and sit in the pew George Washington used to occupy. Then, before they go away, all visitors sign their names in the registry book. It makes a sort of record, you know."

"Oh, I see!" exclaimed Nan, now beginning to understand what he meant. "Once we all went to a historical place with Daddy and Mother, and they signed their names in a book like that and put our names in it, too. I forget just where the place was, though."

"I think it was Washington's headquarters," said Bert.

"That's the kind of a book you will find in Old Church. All visitors sign it," went on the muskrat-hunter. "Maybe the captain's wife and daughter have been at the church, and put down their names and addresses."

"Say, that's a good idea!" exclaimed Bert.

"The only trouble is," spoke Nan, "that the captain thinks his wife may have died, as she wasn't very well. All he hopes to find is his daughter and her children, if she is married and has any."

"Well, then, look for the daughter's name," suggested Mr. Rollin.

"But if she got married her name wouldn't be Van Pelt any longer," Bert suggested.

"That's so," agreed Mr. Rollin. "It isn't going

to be easy to trace her. But if you know the first name of the captain's daughter you might look for that."

"First names are so much alike," said Nan.

"There wouldn't be many names like that of the captain's daughter," exclaimed Bert suddenly. "It was a queer one—he named his schooner after her. It was Debby."

"It couldn't be Debby," said the muskrat-hunter. "That isn't a real name. It must have been Deborah."

"That's it!" exclaimed Nan, her eyes shining with delight. "The captain's daughter was named Deborah and he called her Debby for short."

"Then," suggested Mr. Rollin, "I should say the best thing to do would be to go to Old Church and look for the name Debby, or Deborah. It isn't a common one. There aren't likely to be many. You might make a list of all the Deborahs and their last names. Then the captain can begin his search."

His pony walked along the road through the scrubby evergreens. He turned off the main highway which led to Storm Haven, saying they would get back on it again later.

In a little while the Bobbsey twins reached a small, old-fashioned village. In the heart of it stood a quaint, white church with a parsonage, where the minister lived.

Mr. Rollin knew him. He went to his home and explained the situation to him, and what the Bobbseys wanted to find out.

"I'll show you the visitors' book myself," offered Dr. Crandon. "The sexton isn't in just now. Of course, I know nothing about Captain Van Pelt's people," he added, "but you may find a clue. I hope you do, my dears," he said to the twins.

"It was an attractive old church Even Flossie and Freddie wanted to go in and look at the beautiful stained-glass windows. The "Washington" pew was up front. It had red plush cushions on it, while all the other pew cushions were dark green.

"May we sit in it?" asked Bert in a whisper.

The minister nodded, and the twins seated themselves in a solemn row. Bert and Nan tried to remember everyth.ng they could about Washington, and told the facts to their young brother and sister.

"I should suggest," said Dr. Crandon, "that as the captain's daughter disappeared a long time ago, you look in the front of the book. She could not have been here recently, I think."

With the assistance of the minister, Bert and

Nan looked over the old pages where many names in all sorts of writing were inscribed. Freddie and Flossie meanwhile went out for a walk around the churchyard.

For a time it seemed that no such name as Deborah had ever been written in the book. Then, suddenly, as Nan turned one of the pages she saw something that made her eyes shine brightly.

"There it is!" exclaimed Nan. "There's the name Debby—Deborah Van Pelt. Now we have found the captain's daughter!"

CHAPTER XVII

HELPING THE STOWAWAY

"LET me see, my dear," murmured the minister. "Yes, it's the name Deborah Van Pelt, all right," he admitted. "Well, that is a piece of luck for you."

Nan was so excited that she failed to notice something which Bert picked out.

"The name above it is Van Pelt, too," he said. "See? Hannah Van Pelt. That must have been the captain's wife."

"The address is Centreville," added Dr. Crandon, pointing to the name of the town opposite the word "Van Pelt."

"Where is that place?" asked Nan. "Near here?"

"No," replied the minister. "It's over a hundred miles from here."

"Then we can't go there," said Bert. "Too bad. But we can tell the captain about it when he comes back. Won't he be surprised?"

"I'm sure he'll be very pleased," commented Dr. Crandon.

"We're surely doing something about the mystery now," was Bert's elated comment.

Since there was nothing further that could be found out at Old Church, the Bobbsey twins felt that they had better continue on toward Storm Haven. Bert and Nan, thanking the minister and bidding him good-bye, went outside and found Mr. Rollin telling Flossie and Freddie a story of something that happened once when he went fishing.

"Thank you so much for bringing us here," exclaimed Nan. "You have helped us to find the captain's wife and daughter."

Mr. Rollin was very interested in the story which the older Bobbsey twins told.

"That's splendid," he said. "I'm glad I thought of the record book at Old Church. And I hope the captain finds his people."

The children were driven home in the muskrat-hunter's cart. Mrs. Bobbsey was just beginning to grow worried, for it was late in the afternoon. But she said it was all right for Nan and Bert to have done what they did, and thanked Mr. Rollin for bringing her twins back safely.

"You certainly had an adventure!" exclaimed Mrs. Bobbsey, when she heard about the bear, the wandering of the lost ones, and particularly about the names in the book. "Captain Van Pelt will be very happy to hear about it."

"But it's too late now for me to go selling berries," lamented Bert.

"Never mind," his mother told him. "We'll put them down in the cellar where they will keep fresh and cool. You may try your luck tomorrow."

"I'd rather find Captain Van Pelt's daughter and maybe her little boy or girl, if she has one, than sell berries," said Nan.

"Well," remarked Bert, "you haven't a sailboat as I have and you don't need new cushions for it. Tomorrow I'm going to sell all the berries we picked and get some money."

"You're not going to sell my berries!" decided Freddie.

"Nor mine!" added Flossie.

"No, we'll make yours into pies," laughed Mrs Bobbsey.

When Dinah heard about the bear, she exclaimed:

"Oh, mah goodness! I wish dat I had been wif yo' all t' drive away de b'ar whut wanted t' eat mah honey lambs!"

"I guess the dog scared him off, Dinah," said Freddie.

"Ho! I'd a skairt him mo' as any dorg!" declared the cook.

"Sure you would have!" said Freddie.

The next day Bert rigged up a tray on his bicycle and started out to sell his huckleberries. It was not the first time he had peddled things, for he had done it before when on summer vacations. He stopped at a house, went around to the back door, and asked the lady who opened it if she wanted any berries.

"Not today, little boy," she said, hardly giving Bert a chance to tell her how fine and fresh his fruit was. "My husband doesn't like huckleberry pie."

The lady shut the door. Bert was disappointed but not discouraged. At the second house he sold one quart. At the next two places he had no luck, but at the fifth house the lady bought two quarts.

"I'm doing pretty well," Bert thought. "I wonder how it would be to try the hotel? I think I I will."

As members of the summer cottage colony at Storm Haven, Bert and the other twins had often visited the hotel, going in through the front entrance as did the guests. Bert knew that he was now a peddler selling berries, and realized that nice peddlers do not go to the front entrance of any building to sell their wares.

"I'll have to go around the back way," Bert decided. He went in the side entrance and walked on to the kitchen.

As it happened, the housekeeper was there looking around to make sure that everything was being taken care of, when she saw Bert and his basket of fruit.

"Just what I wanted!" she exclaimed. "One of our guests was asking me why we didn't have more huckleberry pie for dessert and I couldn't answer him. Now I can give him all he wants. I'll take all the berries you have."

"Oh, thank you!" Bert exclaimed. This was very good luck.

The berries were emptied into a big pan and the housekeeper said:

"Now you wait here a moment and I'll get one of the managers to come with the money to pay you. There's no need for you to send a bill for such a small item. Wait here."

You may be very sure Bert would do that very thing. He liked to collect cash for what he sold. Besides, he had almost enough now for one cushion for his sailboat, the *Fairy*. He had seen the

cushions in a store up town that sold marine sup-
plies. They were stuffed with straw and were not
expensive.

In a little while the housekeeper returned with a
young man who was the assistant manager. He
paid Bert, and as the boy was turning back to his
bicycle he heard the young man ask the housekeeper:

"Have you found any young woman entertainer
yet?"

"No, I haven't," she answered. "I've been trying
to locate some girl or young lady who can play the
piano and sing. We'll need one for the children's
masquerade party in a few weeks. I heard of one
young lady who could play the piano, but she
couldn't sing. Then I had another who could sing
but couldn't play. I don't want to hire two. I want
an entertainer who can both play and sing."

"Yes, it would be better to get somebody like
that," the manager agreed. "Well, I guess you'll
just have to keep on looking."

Suddenly Bert had an idea. He remembered
Miss Perkin, the stowaway who wore boys' clothes
She had told the children she could sing and play,
and that she had wanted a position. Here was a
chance, if she was still in Storm Haven.

"Excuse me," said the boy, going back to the kitchen entrance where the manager and housekeeper were still standing, "but I think I know somebody who could entertain for you."

"Do you?" asked the manager, who liked Bert's sparkling eyes and bronzed face. "Is she a young woman?"

"Yes, sir."

"And can she both sing and play the piano?" asked the housekeeper.

"She told us she could," Bert said. "She didn't play the piano when she was stowed away with us on Captain Van Pelt's ship because he had no piano. But she sang."

"What do you mean, she was a stowaway?" asked the manager.

"Oh, she just went on board and fell asleep," Bert said.

"Well, that might happen to anyone," chuckled the manager. "But tell us more about this young lady, my boy."

This Bert did, glad of a chance to help the stowaway. He said he would take word to her to come to the hotel to let them hear her sing and play. Bert suddenly thought of something that made him hestitate.

"Maybe she wouldn't be stylish enough for you," he said.

"What do you mean—stylish?" asked the house-keeper. "Any well-dressed young lady would be all right."

"Well," said Bert, "that's just the trouble. You see, she wears boys' clothes!"

CHAPTER XVIII

FREDDIE'S BIG FISH

SOMEWHAT surprised at what Bert had said, the manager and housekeeper looked at each other. Bert felt that he must tell the truth about Miss Perkin.

"Boys' clothes!" exclaimed the housekeeper.

"Do you mean she wears them on the street?" asked the manager. "Or when she is playing some part in an entertainment? Of course, if she takes the part of a boy——"

"No," said Bert, determined to make it plain, "she uses them on the street, and she wore them on Captain Van Pelt's ship."

"Well, if Captain Van Pelt, who is one of our guests when he comes to Storm Haven, doesn't object to this young lady having boys' clothes," said the housekeeper, "it might be all right to consider her."

The woman was in a hurry to get some one.

"I don't see how we could have her sit at the

155

piano and sing to the guests in that sort of a costume," objected the manager.

"No, I guess you're right," said the housekeeper. "I'm afraid your friend will not do, my boy. I'm sorry."

"But," exclaimed Bert, who began to see the chances of Miss Perkin getting work growing dim, "I guess she wears them only when she's fly-casting. She is an expert fly-caster and wants to give lessons, but she can't find anybody who wants to learn, and she hasn't any money left, and——"

"Oh, if she only wears boys' clothes when fly-casting, that's different," said the manager, smiling. "I have seen a number of lady fly-casters in coats and trousers," he added.

"Of course, that's different," agreed the housekeeper with a laugh. "I suppose she wouldn't want to do any fly-casting in the hotel," she said to Bert.

"I guess not," he replied, smiling.

"You tell your friend to come to the hotel to see me," suggested the assistant manager. "Tell her to ask for Mr. Blake."

"And be sure to have her wear a nice dress when she comes here!" added the housekeeper.

"I'll tell her!" promised Bert.

As he hopped onto his bicycle, the money from

the sale of his huckleberries jingled in his pocket.

His first thought was to ride at once to the cottage where Miss Perkin boarded and tell her the good news. Then, thinking that Nan might like to share in the message, Bert rode home. After putting away the berry money until he could get more to buy a set of cushions for his boat, he called to his twin sister.

"Oh!" exclaimed Nan in delight. "It was good of you to come and take me, Bert. It will be wonderful news for her, I'm sure."

"If she only won't wear boys' clothes," said Bert.

"Don't worry—she won't," spoke Mrs. Bobbsey with a laugh.

Bert and his sister found Miss Perkin, still wearing trousers, working in the yard back of the cottage. She had a fish-pole and was flicking a line into some barrel hoops laid on the ground. With a swish and a hum the weight on the end of the line fell almost in the centre of each hoop, one after the other. Fascinated, Bert and Nan watched for a moment.

"There!" exclaimed Miss Perkin, "I think I did pretty well. Now, if only some one wanted to learn fly-casting—why, it's the Bobbsey twins!" she cried with a smile as she turned and saw Nan and Bert. "Have you come to take me as a stowaway on another voyage?" she asked.

"Not exactly," Bert answered. "But if you'll remove those——"

"Let me tell her," interrupted Nan in a low voice.

This Bert generously did, and Nan told about the opportunity Miss Perkin had of becoming a singing and playing entertainer at the Edgemere Hotel. As she realized what Nan was saying, the stowaway's eyes brightened and her tanned cheeks flushed.

"Oh, what glorious news!" she exclaimed. "Thank you a thousand times, my dears! It was wonderful of you to think of me."

"Bert did that," said Nan. "He went to the hotel to sell berries and heard the manager and the housekeeper talking about needing some one to entertain every day, and also for the children's big party at the end of the season."

"And Bert thought of me. Oh, I could kiss you!" exclaimed Miss Perkin. But Bert got behind Nan.

"Tell her about the boys' clothes," he whispered. "She can't wear them."

But it was not necessary for Nan to explain.

Miss Perkin had heard what Bert said. Then, with a merry laugh, she exclaimed:

"Oh, I shouldn't dream of going to the hotel this way." She looked down at her trousers. "I wear these only when practicing fly-casting or when I'm a stowaway!" And again she laughed.

"Then I guess it will be all right," said Bert.

"I knew it would be," Nan murmured.

"You dear twins!" laughed Miss Perkin, as she insisted on blowing Bert a kiss from her finger tips at least. "I'll go right down to the hotel to see about this job. It has come just in the nick of time. I was going away from here at the end of the week if I didn't get a chance to earn some money."

"That would have been too bad," said Nan.

"And I'll put on my best dress!" the teacher laughed, "and I'll even powder my nose!"

Nan giggled merrily.

Later that day Miss Perkin stopped at Button-ball Cottage to tell Mrs. Bobbsey and the twins that she had been engaged as entertainer at the hotel.

"I played and sang for them," she said, "and they were kind enough to say it was just what they wanted. So if you come to the hotel you'll see me at the piano."

"I'm coming there when they have the masquerade party," said Flossie. "I'm going to dress up like a fairy."

"And I'm coming dressed like a fireman," said Freddie. "No—I forgot—I mean like a sailor. I was going to be a fireman, but I'm going to be a sailor instead. And do you suppose, Mother," he asked, "that I could have Mr. Pegleg Baldwin put some tattooing on me?"

"Oh, no!" gasped Mrs. Bobbsey.

"Sailors have to be tattooed," insisted Freddie.

"Well, you're going to be one sailor who isn't!" said his mother.

The others joined in a general laugh, and then Miss Perkin said:

"While I was at the hotel, I saw a little girl who is in my class at school. I think it would be nice for Flossie to play with her."

"I'd like to," came from the younger Bobbsey girl. "What does she like to do?"

"She is a great swimmer and diver," replied Miss Perkin. "She has won some prizes in diving exhibitions."

"Oh," cried Flossie, "maybe she won't like me, 'cause I can't dive."

The teacher smiled

"She's a very sweet little girl," she said. "It wouldn't make any difference about that."

"Maybe she'll give you some lessons," offered Freddie wisely.

"Just what I was thinking," was Miss Perkin's comment. "Would you like to come with me now, Flossie, and find Marian? She's at the hotel pool most of the time."

Flossie was delighted, and as soon as she received permission from her mother, took hold of the teacher's hand, and started off with the former stowaway.

"Mother," said Nan a few minutes later, "I have been thinking a lot about the names in the book at Old Church, and I was wondering if we couldn't do something about solving the mystery before Captain Van Pelt gets back."

"What have you in mind, dear?" asked Mrs. Bobbsey.

"Couldn't we write to somebody in Centreville," suggested Nan, "and find out if the Van Pelts still live there?"

"I presume so," replied the girl's mother. "Would you like me to send a note to the postmaster? Then if the captain's people have moved away, perhaps he can show my letter to someone who has lived there a long time and might know where the Van Pelts are."

"Oh, Mother," said Nan, "that would be wonderful. Can't we do it right away?"

"All right."

Accordingly, a letter was written explaining what the Bobbseys wanted to know to help out their sailor friend. Nan herself carried the missive to the post office, wondering how long they would have to wait for an answer.

In the meantime, the twins were awaiting a short vacation which their father hoped to spend with them.

Mr. Bobbsey intended to spend two weeks at the shore. The children had prepared to do so much for this period that Mrs. Bobbsey said her husband would need to be four men to take it all in.

One scheme that was carried out, however, was when Mr. Bobbsey took the children onto the bay for a fishing trip. He hired a large rowboat, and with poles and lines, a basket of lunch, and another basket to hold the fish that might be caught, the little party started out. Mrs. Bobbsey did not go along.

"Bring me home some fish, honey lambs!" Dinah called to them as they departed.

"I'll bring the biggest one!" boasted Freddie.

"Just watch me!" chuckled Bert.

Mr. Bobbsey and Bert rowed the boat out to where the bay merged into the ocean, and the water was a bit rough and deep. By this time the Bobbsey twins were all good sailors and knew something about fishing.

"Now, where do you think there is a good fishing place?" asked Mr. Bobbsey of Bert. "You've been down here at Storm Haven longer than I have. Did you hear any of the sailors, fishermen, or lobstermen say where there was a good spot?"

Bert recalled that once, while taking a sailing lesson from Bill Radder, the man had indicated a place outside one of the points of the harbor. Storm Haven harbor was shaped something like a crescent moon, the two points being strips of land extending well out into the bay where the rough ocean met and joined with the calmer waters. One of these was called "South Point."

"Bill Radder said that off 'South Point' there are good fishing grounds," announced Bert.

"Then we'll go there," decided the father of the Bobbsey twins.

"It's a bit rough," warned Bert.

"Well, we have a good, safe boat."

He and his older boy rowed the boat out toward South Point. There the anchor was again let down over the side, the rope running out from where it had been coiled in the bow.

"It's a bit deep here," Mr. Bobbsey said, noticing how much of the anchor rope ran out.

"Then we ought to catch plenty of big fish," Bert remarked. "Big fish live in deep water."

"Here's where I'll get the one for Dinah to cook," said Freddie, fixing his pole and line. Flossie decided that she did not want to fish, so she curled up near her father, who was at the stern, and looked at some picture papers Mr. Bobbsey had in his pocket.

Nan was almost as enthusiastic about fishing as was Bert, and the two older twins, with Freddie and Mr. Bobbsey, soon had their hooks baited once more and had cast in.

Hardly had Bert's hook and sinker gone below the surface than his reel began to hum shrilly.

"I've hooked one!" he cried.

"Don't let him get away!" called his father.

A moment later, while Bert was reeling in his fish, Nan cried:

"I have a bite!"

"Then I guess we came to the right place."

He waited until Bert had pulled in his fish before paying much attention to his own line. Bert's catch was a good-sized one, though it could not be called big. Nan had hooked one that looked about the same as her brother's. Suddenly Freddie set up a great shout.

"I have a big fish!" he yelled.

But it was not as large as Nan's or Bert's. However, Freddie said this was only a "practice" fish, and that he would soon get another.

A moment later Mr. Bobbsey caught a really fine fry, and from that time on the luck of the Bobbsey fishing party was very good. The basket began to fill up, and when Nan caught a larger fish than had either her father or Bert, she laughed merrily.

It was when Mr. Bobbsey was ready to announce that they had enough, that Freddie provided the sensation of the day. The tip of the small boy's pole suddenly bent in a bow, his reel spun very fast, and he cried:

"Now I've caught a big one! A great big one!"

He was very excited.

"I believe he has, Dad!" shouted Bert. "He has a regular whale! Look at it pull! Wait, Freddie, I'll help you!"

Nan was exclaiming with delight at her little brother's success, and Flossie was screaming in her excitement. The boat was in a commotion.

"Steady!" called Mr. Bobbsey. "Don't upset us, children!"

CHAPTER XIX

A STRANGE FIND

BERT BOBBSEY came to the aid of his brother just in time. Freddie had really hooked such a big fish that the small chap would have had trouble in getting it into the boat by himself. Both boys had hold of the pole, but Bert was winding in the line on the reel. The fish fought and tried to hold back, but the tackle was strong, and slowly the prize catch was hauled nearer and nearer the side of the boat.

"Oh, he's a whopper!" yelled Freddie. "You'd better get him in the rest of the way for me, Bert. Just look! What a whopper!"

Freddie's fish was, indeed, a large one. In order to see it better, the little boy leaned over the side of the craft, just beneath the edge of which the fish was still splashing and trying to pull away from Bert.

"Oh, I've caught the biggest fish!" Freddie yelled.

A moment later he went head-first over the side of the boat, which was bobbing about in the rough water.

"Look! Look! Freddie's overboard!" screamed Nan.

"Steady now, everybody!" commanded Mr. Bobbsey. "Sit still, or you'll upset the boat. I'll get Freddie!"

"Help me get him back in, Bert!" called his father.

By this time Bert had hauled the big fish over the side, and the creature was flopping and flipping about on the bottom of the craft. Mr. Bobbsey reached over the side and grasped Freddie. Slowly Bert and Mr. Bobbsey pulled the little boy into the boat. Then suddenly there came another splash.

"Has anybody else fallen in?" asked Mr. Bobbsey, looking over his shoulder to where Nan and Flossie were sitting.

"It's our basket of fish!" exclaimed Nan. "The whole thing went over the side! Look!"

It was true enough. The commotion in the boat had caused it to tilt, and as the basket of fish was on one of the seats it was an easy matter for it to slide overboard. The little receptacle floated along, but all the fish, some of them still alive, either sank or swam away.

"Well, things happened very suddenly," said Mr. Bobbsey. "Now don't cry, Freddie," he added. "You're all right."

"But my fish! My big fish! Where's the big fish I caught?" wailed the little chap.

"Your fish is safe," Bert answered. "It's in the boat. It's the only one we have left of all those we caught."

"No matter," said Mr. Bobbsey. "This big one Freddie caught will make more than a meal for us. Why, it's a fine bluefish!" he added. "It's the only one caught today. Freddie, you did great!"

"I told you I'd catch a big fish!" said Freddie, his sobs lessening, now that the danger and his fear had passed. "Say, he *is* big, isn't he?" he murmured, as he saw the flapping creature in the bottom of the boat.

"Couldn't be better," Mr. Bobbsey said. "Now I think we'll pull up the anchor and go back home to get Freddie dried out. We'll have Dinah bake his bluefish for dinner."

"You can all eat some," Freddie said generously.

"Well, we might as well save the basket," remarked Bert, reaching to it with the boat hook.

The fishing party was soon rowing toward the beach nearest to Buttonball Cottage. Freddie, dripping wet, was mounting guard over his fish—the only one left of all that had been caught.

Mrs. Bobbsey was much surprised when her husband and the children returned. She knew at a glance that something had happened.

"You poor little fellow!" she said to Freddie, clasping him, wet as he was, in her arms.

"Oh, I'm all right," he said. "Look at my big fish. I want to show it to Dinah."

"But Freddie," said his mother, who could hardly keep from laughing at the way her little boy looked. "Did *you* catch that big fish?"

"Yes," said Freddie proudly. "And we're going to eat him for dinner tonight."

"That will be fine," said his mother.

It was so long that the tail dragged on the floor as Freddie, straining hard, carried it to the kitchen to show the cook.

"Mah good lan' ob massy!" cried Dinah in astonishment. "Who caught dat shark?"

"I caught him!" laughed Freddie. "But it isn't a shark—it's a bluefish."

"An' yo' ole Dinah she sho' know how t' cook it fo' her honey lambs!" chuckled the fat Negro.

"But did yo' all hab t' jump in de ocean t' cotch dat fish, Freddie?" she asked.

"No, I just fell in," Freddie said.

As Dinah began to fix the big fish, the young angler went upstairs to put on some dry clothes. Meanwhile Nan, Bert, and Mr. Bobbsey told Mrs. Bobbsey of the adventures of the day.

"I have a surprise to tell, too," said the twins' mother. "A very pleasant surprise."

"Did you receive a letter?" asked Nan quickly.

"Yes," replied Mrs. Bobbsey, going to a desk and picking up a large envelope. "This is an answer from an old man who has lived in Centreville all his life."

"What does he say?" asked Bert and Nan together.

The message was read aloud.

"Dear Mrs. Bobbsey: Our postmaster gave me your letter, asking for information about Mrs. Hannah Van Pelt and her daughter Deborah. I guess they are the people you are looking for, because the woman's husband was a sea captain and was lost a good many years ago.

"The mother and daughter lived here a good many years—in fact, Debby as we called the little girl, grew up here. Then they moved to New

York. Some time later I received an announcement of Debby's marriage. I can't remember the man's name, but it seems to me it was Denton.

"I haven't heard of the Van Pelts since, but I hope this information will help you. I should like to hear if this family gets reunited.

Yours very truly,

John Clark."

"Oh, Mother," exclaimed Nan, dancing around the room, "isn't this wonderful news!"

"You Bobbseys are pretty good detectives," laughed the father of the twins. "But the mystery isn't solved yet. However, Captain Van Pelt will certainly be glad to learn this much."

While the family were still rejoicing over the good news, they were startled to have Dinah suddenly appear from the kitchen, very much excited, and exclaiming:

"Look! Look! See whut I done found inside de fish Freddie cotched!"

"Is it a diamond?" asked Nan, remembering a story she had once read about a jewel being found inside a fish.

"No, 'tisn't perzackly a diamond," Dinah answered. "But it's gold an' it sparkles. I guess it's a sort ob locket."

"Do you mean to say you found that inside the bluefish?" asked Mr. Bobbsey.

"Right inside when I was cleanin' him!" declared the cook. "Mah knife gritted on suffin' hard, an' when I looked I found dis in de stomach ob Freddie's fish!"

She held out a strange find.

CHAPTER XX

A DANGEROUS DIVE

THEY all clustered around Dinah, looking at the shining object in her black hand.

"Was that really inside the fish I caught?" asked Freddie.

"It sho' was, honey lamb," she answered.

"What is it?" asked Bert.

"It's some sort of a locket, or charm, such as a man might wear on his watch chain," said Mr. Bobbsey, taking it from Dinah. She had wiped it clean before bringing it in. Mr. Bobbsey examined it closely. "Yes, it's a charm for a chain," he went on, "and I think it is meant to be opened."

"Can you open it and see if there is anything inside?" asked Mrs. Bobbsey. "Perhaps if there is a name or a picture in it we can find out to whom it belongs."

"These watch chain charms," said Mr. Bobbsey, as he took out his knife with which to open the hinged bit of gold, "were generally made to hold little pictures. I don't know whether there is one in here or not."

"And to think that it came out of the stomach of a fish!" murmured Mrs. Bobbsey. "How long do you suppose it has been in there, Dick?"

"There is no way of telling," he answered. "I should say, though, that this charm has been inside the fish quite a long time. It is worn smooth on the outside, which would be caused by its being rubbed by the things the fish ate and digested. It couldn't digest the charm as it is of metal, and won't dissolve."

"Where did the fish get it?" asked Flossie. "Did he eat some man who had this locket on his watch chain?"

"A bluefish, even as large as the one Freddie caught, could never eat a man," said Mr. Bobbsey with a laugh. "He couldn't even eat a boy. What I think happened was, that whoever owned this charm must have dropped it into the water while leaning over the edge of a dock or over the side of a boat or ship. The locket fell to the bottom of the bay, perhaps even to the bottom of the sea, where the fish found and swallowed it."

"I guess he thought it was something good to eat," laughed Freddie.

"Very likely," agreed his father. "Or the charm might have been mixed in some food the bluefish swallowed. At any rate, I'll try to open it to see what's inside."

After two attempts, working carefully with his knife so he would not scratch the gold charm, Mr. Bobbsey finally managed to force apart the two hinged halves. So tightly did they fit that no water had seeped inside.

"What is it?" asked Nan, as her father stood looking at what was revealed.

"It's some sort of a picture," he answered.

"Only one picture?" asked Mrs. Bobbsey. "Usually there are two in a charm of that kind, one in each half."

"There is only one picture here," said Mr. Bobbsey. "It is the photograph of a little girl about Flossie's age, I should judge. Wait a moment!" he exclaimed, taking the locket to the light. "There are two pictures here after all, one in each side. One of them is so dim and faded that I cannot make out what it is. It might be that of a lady. The other, which is quite plain, is probably that of the owner's daughter. Well, well! How strange!"

The twins crowded about their father to look at the face of the little girl in the charm. As Mr.

Bobbsey had said, the other picture was merely a shadow, the face dim and blurred. Yet that of the little girl was quite clear.

It was the likeness of a child, as Mr. Bobbsey had remarked, about Flossie's own age. She had long curls, and was smiling a little.

"She is wearing an old-fashioned dress," said Nan. "That picture must have been taken many years ago—oh, Bert!"

For a moment the older twins stared at each other, saying nothing. Then Bert exclaimed:

"I've seen a picture like that before, some place."

"So have I!" agreed Nan.

"But I can't seem to remember the place," went on Bert.

"I can," suddenly cried Nan. "Don't you recall, Bert? Captain Van Pelt showed us photographs of his wife and little girl one day."

"Yes, I remember now," Bert agreed.

"Well," went on Nan, turning to her father and mother, "this is like the picture of his little girl the captain showed us. It's his daughter as she was then, a good many years ago. Maybe this other picture that has faded was that of his wife."

"Say, he'll certainly be glad to see this again!"

"Oh, when is he coming back?" asked Nan. "We have so much to tell him."

"Soon. Very soon," replied Mr. Bobbsey. "But wait a moment. You don't want to make a mistake. It would be too bad to tell the captain that we had found his daughter's picture in a locket, only to have it turn out that it isn't so at all. Are you sure this is like the picture he showed you?"

Nan and Bert were both certain of it. They remembered particularly the little girl's curls and her old-fashioned dress.

"Do you think, Dick," asked Mrs. Bobbsey, "that Captain Van Pelt could have been in this neighborhood many years ago and lost the locket in the water?"

"No, I hardly think that," was the answer. "If such had been the case the captain would have mentioned it to Bert and Nan. What I believe happened was that someone else had this charm which, at one time, may have been on the captain's watch chain."

"Then," spoke Bert, "some one around here must have known the captain well to have had his charm with his little girl's picture."

"Yes," said his father, "and no. You see, blue-fish are great travellers. However, it seems likely that some trace of Captain Van Pelt's people can be found right around here."

"I can hardly wait to see the captain," said Nan.

She did have to wait for several days, nevertheless. In the meantime, she and Bert made a trip to the huckleberry patch near the muskrat-hunter's cabin. They did not see Sim Rollins, but they did fill two large pails with huckleberries, and after Dinah had taken all she wanted for some pies and a pudding, Bert sold the rest.

"Now I have enough money for my boat cushions," he said to his twin. "I'll buy them and pretty soon I'll take you for a sail, Nan."

"All by ourselves?" she asked.

"Sure! I'm getting to know how to sail pretty well. Mr. Radder says I'm learning fast. He's given me several lessons. One more, and then I can go all over the bay by myself. Then I'm going to practice for the race."

"Oh, do you expect to take part in the hotel race?" asked Nan.

"Yes, in the junior class," Bert said. "That's for boys under twelve. I can just qualify, and I hope I'll win."

"I hope so, too," agreed Nan.

The next day, when Flossie had gone with Freddie to the hotel lagoon where he wanted to sail his toy boat, the little "fat fairy" came running home, quite excited.

"Where's my bathing suit, Mother?" she called.

"What do you want with it?" asked Mrs. Bobbsey.

"That nice girl Marian is at the pool," said Flossie, "and she is going to teach me how to dive. I know how to swim but I don't know how to dive, and she's going to show me."

"Well, all right," Mrs. Bobbsey said. "She's the one Miss Perkin introduced to you, isn't she? But you'd better go with your sister, Nan. Flossie is a good swimmer for her age, but diving is something different. Make sure this little girl knows what she is doing."

The children could dress in the cottage and walk either to the beach or to the hotel pool in their swimming costumes. So both Nan and Flossie put on their bathing suits.

"I'll go watch you learn how to dive," Nan said. "Then I think I may as well have a swim myself."

"Yes, do," agreed Flossie.

As the two girls reached the hotel pool where many ladies and children were disporting themselves in the water, Flossie pointed to a high platform at one end—the diving platform—and said:

"There's Marian now. She's going to make a high dive."

Nan saw a little girl, somewhat older than Flossie, clad in a bright red suit, and poised on the edge of the diving board. She was a graceful little figure and seemed perfectly at ease in her elevated position. She seemed to be known to some of the hotel patrons and guests, and several swimmers paused to watch her dive.

"That child is a perfect marvel!" Nan heard one lady say.

"Yes," agreed another, "I never saw anyone like her. Does she live around here?"

"Yes, I believe she and her mother have a cottage somewhere back of Storm Haven," was the answer. "I've often seen the little girl around the hotel, but her mother rarely comes. She is not very well, I believe."

"How sad! But there's nothing of the invalid about Marian."

"No, indeed. Now watch her, for she is going to dive!"

Marian, as many divers do, paused for just the right moment before making the long plunge.

"That's the girl who's going to teach me to

dive," Flossie whispered to Nan. "Sometime I'll be able to jump off like she does."

"Oh, you wouldn't dare," Nan said.

Just then Marian leaned forward in the last motion before making the dive. As she did so, a man on the concrete edge of the pool, almost beneath the diving platform, stepped out where he could see the child and cried:

"Wait! Wait! Don't dive! It's dangerous!"

But it was too late.

The little body, clad in the red bathing suit, was falling through the air toward the water.

CHAPTER XXI

GOOD NEWS

ALARMED by the warning cries of the man, several women screamed. Some of them saw the same danger to the little diver that the man had, and they added their cries to his.

Then Nan saw what the danger was.

Many children, some of them hotel guests, others living at the summer resort cottages, played, swam and dived at the hotel pool every fine day. There was a large crowd present. Several of them had inflated rubber toys in the shape of horses, fish, seals, and other beasts. On these they could lie, sit, or paddle with their hands and feet around the shallow end of the pool and down to the deep end where the diving platforms had been erected.

Besides the toys of floating rubber animals, there were some in the form of miniature rafts which were quite bulky and heavy. It was one of these that had floated down to the deep end without anyone on it. It lay directly in the path of

Marian s dive. It was not there when she leaped off the platform, but floated into place after she had left it. She was therefore in great danger of hitting it.

Diving from a height is always more or less hazardous. If a person strikes a solid object in the water there is even greater danger. This was what little Marian in her red suit was likely to do.

The man who had shouted the warning did more than that. When he saw that his cry was too late and that Marian had leaped from the high platform, he caught up a bamboo pole used by the swimming-master in supporting new and timid swimmers, and with this pushed the floating raft out of the way.

He was only just in time, for a second later Marian's little body struck the water, disappeared beneath it, then came gracefully up in a long curve. Brushing the water from her eyes, the young swimmer got to the edge of the pool and climbed out. The excitement and danger were over almost before those present could realize it.

"My, but that was a narrow escape!" exclaimed one of the ladies.

"Indeed it was," agreed a friend.

"Clever work. Mr. Martin," said the swimming-master to the gentleman who had pushed the raft out of the way. "I must caution the boys and girls about letting their toys float down to this end of the pool."

Marian climbed out laughing, and ran to greet Flossie. She did not realize that she had just escaped serious injury.

"Oh, I'm so glad you've come!" she said to Flossie. "Will you go diving with me?"

"I think she'll have to learn quite a bit before she can dive with you," said Nan. "You are an expert."

Nan knew something about diving. Her father had shown her a little about it when he had taught her and Freddie to swim. But Flossie had never cared much about jumping head-first into the water. Now that she had seen Marian do it, however, she grew bolder and was soon leaping in, trying to stand, hold herself, and imitate Laura.

"She could have no better teacher," said Mr. Rowland, the swimming instructor at the pool "What children need most of all, in learning to swim and dive, is confidence. Marian will be the best teacher Flossie could ever have."

Nan watched the two for a while. Then, assuring herself that Flossie would be safe, since the swim-.

ming-master was on hand, and relying on Marian's judgment in not leading Flossie into too deep water, she went swimming and diving by herself. She did caution Flossie on one point, however.

"You mustn't jump off the high dive," said Nan.

"I won't," Flossie promised. "But may I after Marian has given me some lessons?"

"I'll see," said Nan.

"All right."

"She seems like a nice little playmate for you," remarked Nan. "Have a good time."

This Flossie did, and when noon came and it was time to go home for lunch she had progressed considerably in learning how to dive.

"I'm going to take lots of lessons from Marian," Flossie said when she walked along with Nan. "And we're going to the children's masquerade together."

"That will be nice," Nan agreed.

"Marian says she is going to wear one of her mother's dresses," went on Flossie.

"Her mother's dress!" exclaimed Nan. "Won't it be too big for her, Flossie?"

"Oh, I mean it's a dress Marian's mother wore when she was a little girl," went on Flossie.

The following day Captain Van Pelt anchored

at Storm Haven. Although Mr. Bobbsey had left
for the city he had not seen the old sailor, as he
had had other business to which to attend.

"Then we can be the first to tell the captain the
good news," said Nan, who was so excited she
could hardly wait for their friend to be rowed to
shore by Pegleg Baldwin.

"You saw his daughter's name first in the book,"
remarked Bert, who was walking up and down the
dock with his twin, "so I suppose you ought to be
the one to tell him."

"You pulled in Freddie's fish," responded Nan,
"so you must tell him about the locket."

As it happened, neither Bobbsey stuck to his
own story. The captain was told in such a jumbled
way what the children had found out that he was
completely bewildered.

"What's this I hear?" he asked. "My daughter's
picture was inside a fish, and she went to an old
church and married a man named Denton!"

The twins had to laugh when they realized that
they had not been telling their story very well.

"You'd better let me talk first, Bert," said Nan.

"Oh, all right," agreed her brother. "But hurry
up. I want Captain Van Pelt to hear about the
locket."

"I think you both had better come to the hotel with me," advised the captain. "We can sit down there and I can get this story straight."

When this had been done, and all that the Bobbsey family had found out had been told to the old seaman, and he had been given the locket by Bert, he was very happy; in fact, he said he would start out the next morning to try to trace his lost relatives.

"But I don't know whether to stay around Storm Haven to search," he pondered, "or go to New York to look up people named Denton."

Bert had a suggestion to offer.

CHAPTER XXII

A NICE REWARD

NAN BOBBSEY looked at her brother to hear what suggestion he was about to offer.

"Captain Van Pelt," said Bert, "why don't you go to New York to find out what you can about your relatives, and let Nan and me keep on looking around here?"

"That's a splendid idea," replied the old sailor "You're the most wonderful children I've ever met I don't know what I should have done without you."

Bert and Nan smiled, but were too modest to agree with him.

"We're glad to have been able to help you," said Nan, "and we're going to keep on until this mystery is solved."

The twins left the old man to his thoughts, and hurried to Buttonball Cottage.

A few days later Bert said to Nan:

"I'd like to take Dad out in the sailboat when

he comes down tomorrow. Do you think he would go?"

"Perhaps," replied his sister. "But I imagine he'd rather go fishing in a rowboat."

Her statement proved to be true, Moreover, there was not one bit of wind, so a sailing trip would have had to have been postponed, anyway. The four twins were to go with their father, but Freddie was the most enthusiastic of all the young anglers.

"I'm going to hook another big fish," he boasted.

"I s'pose you think there'll be a treasure in it," said Flossie.

"Anyway, we'll have a good dinner."

As it happened, it was Bert who was to get a big catch this time, but the kind of a haul it proved to be was nothing like the one his small brother had made. It would be hard to decide, however, which one was the more surprising.

For a time after they had anchored their boat, their luck was not very good. Only a few small fish were caught, and Mr. Bobbsey was thinking of pulling up and moving to a better location, when Bert hooked into something which felt quite large and heavy on the end of his line.

"Oh, it's a big fish!" cried Nan.

"No, it doesn't feel like a fish," Bert said.

Then slowly he drew up from the waves a strange object.

"Oh, what is it?" cried Nan.

"It's nothing but a bunch of seaweed," Flossie declared, as a mass of the green stuff came into view at the surface of the water.

"There's some seaweed all right," spoke Mr. Bobbsey. "But there's more than that. Bert, I think perhaps you've hooked something worthwhile."

Bert pulled hard, and in a moment a heavy object landed in the boat with a thump. It was so covered with the dripping seaweed that the Bobbseys could not figure out what it might be.

"Maybe it's a great big clam," said Freddie.

"If it is, don't let it bite me," begged Flossie.

"Clams don't bite, but lobsters pinch you," said her small brother.

"Well, don't let it pinch me, then," begged the little girl.

By this time Bert and his father were pulling apart the bunch of seaweed from which a little puddle of water was spreading over the bottom boards of the craft. In the midst of the green mass lay what Bert had pulled up from beneath the green waves.

"There it is!" cried Nan, as the sun gleamed on something shiny.

"It's brass," said Freddie.

"It's a brass box!" added Flossie.

As Mr. Bobbsey and Bert pulled off more and more of the seaweed the object could be seen more plainly.

"It isn't all a brass box," said Bert. "It's a wooden box with brass strips around it."

Then in an instant he and Nan knew what had been dragged up from the depths of the bay.

"It's Captain Van Pelt's treasure box!" shouted Bert.

"That's just what it is," agreed Nan joyfully.

"It doesn't seem possible," remarked their father, "but it surely is a brass-bound box of some sort. It has a small handle on each end. Your hook caught in one of them, Bert."

"It's the captain's treasure chest, all right," went on Bert, when all the seaweed had been cleaned off and the box had been placed upon a seat in the boat. "He'll be very glad to get it back."

"Won't he, though!" agreed Nan. "Now he can show us the things that are inside of it—the treasures he was saving for his daughter, and any grandchildren he might have and not know about."

"I'm afraid," said Mr. Bobbsey, "that whatever is in this box is spoiled by the sea water."

"No, Dad," said Bert, "it's a water-tight box, so the captain said."

"Well, maybe the contents will be all right. But it certainly is a remarkable and lucky coincidence that you hooked into it, Bert."

"How do you suppose it got out here when the wave swept it away near the hotel beach?" asked Nan.

"The tide must have carried it along on the bottom of the bay," said Mr. Bobbsey.

"Well," remarked Bert, as he held up the box to get a better look at it, "then it's a lucky thing we happened to anchor in this place."

"Yes," agreed his father, "it is. It hasn't been such a good spot for fish, but it's an excellent place for treasure."

The box was safely stowed away in one of the lockers of the boat, and the wet, slimy seaweed was tossed overboard. Then Mr. Bobbsey said:

"I think we might as well move along and try to catch fish. We aren't having any luck here."

Although the Bobbsey twins and their father spent several hours on the water, they could not be said to have kept their minds on their fishing.

Every few minutes one of them would speak about the wonderful luck that had come to them in locating the old sailor's property.

"I think we should see Captain Van Pelt as soon as we get home," said Nan.

"Sure," agreed Bert. "I'll carry his chest over to the hotel."

"Didn't you tell me," asked Mr. Bobbsey wisely, "that he was going away to find out something about his relatives?"

"That's right," replied Nan. "But maybe he'll be back by this time."

As soon as Mrs. Bobbsey had been told of the unusual happening of the day, she urged the children, at least the older twins, to go to the hotel to inquire for Captain Van Pelt.

They set off at once, Bert carrying the box. When they reached the Edgemere, they found to their disappointment that Captain Van Pelt had not returned.

"We have something we wanted to give him," said Bert to the desk clerk, setting down the treasure box, which was wrapped up.

"Oh, let me take charge of it," the clerk said. "I will lock it in our safe and it will be all right. Captain Van Pelt is sure to be back in a day or so, or at least within the week. His schooner is still out in the bay."

As the Bobbseys turned to go down the steps, they spied a familiar figure coming up the walk.

"It's Captain Van Pelt!" cried Bert. "Now we can give him his treasure."

"He looks kind of sad, though," whispered Nan. "Maybe he has had bad news. Perhaps he won't need his treasure."

CHAPTER XXIII

PREPARING FOR A PARTY

As BERT and Nan watched the sea captain come up the walk, they hardly knew what to say to him. They wanted to tell him at once about the treasure chest which they had found, feeling sure that fact would make him happy. However, he seemed to be sad, so they decided to wait for him to speak first.

Something happened just then which made it unnecessary for them to have worried. With a dash Freddie Bobbsey came sliding around the side of the hotel porch, made a flying leap from the steps, and landed directly in front of Captain Van Pelt.

"Oh—we found—your treasure!" exclaimed the small boy breathlessly. "And it was in the seaweed. Bert pulled it up."

By this time Flossie had arrived from the same direction and began talking, as she brushed back her curls.

"Will you show us what's inside your wooden chest?" she asked. "You said you would."

The captain looked startled. Then he began to laugh.

"Is this really true?" he asked, looking at the older twins who had walked up to him.

"Yes, it is," Bert informed him. "Your treasure chest is in the safe in the hotel office."

"Well, I declare!" said the captain. "That's splendid. You must tell me all about it."

They went up to the man's room, and there he heard the full story of the finding of the box. Then he opened it and showed its contents to the children.

Everything in it was unharmed from the water in which the box had been immersed. The children exclaimed over the quaint but simple treasures the captain had collected on his different voyages. There were gold and silver ornaments, rings, bangles, bracelets, and many curios of the sea.

"Oh, what beautiful things!" gasped Nan. "That necklace——"

"That came from China," the captain told her.

"And that gorgeous bracelet and the earrings to match," said Nan. "Mother once told me those stones are called amethysts."

"I like those red beads," said Bert. "I mean for a girl," he added quickly.

"I bought those in South America," explained Captain Van Pelt. "By the way, speaking of South America, that's why I came back here."

"Did you—did you hear that your wife—and daughter—were there?" asked Nan, almost afraid to inquire.

"No. No, I didn't," replied the old sailor, shaking his head. "I had word I have to start for South America day after tomorrow to get a load of lumber, so I must get my crew together."

There was a pause, and the Bobbseys were too polite to ask any more questions.

"I suppose you'd like to hear about what I learned in Centreville and New York," the captain said slowly. "I wish I had more to tell you than I have. I did find out enough, from the clues you gave me, to make me sure I can locate my daughter some time."

"Your daughter?" asked Nan. "You mean——"

"I was told by some people in Centreville that my wife died several years ago," the man replied. "I was afraid she had."

"But Debby—I mean Mrs. Denton," said Bert. "Did you find out where she is?"

"A woman I met thought that my daughter's husband was working for one of the big insurance companies in New York," the captain went on, "so I am trying to find my Debby by that means. But it takes time. Then too, the woman who gave me the information may be wrong."

"Oh, we hope you find your daughter," said Flossie.

"I'm sure you will some time," put in Nan kindly.

"Perhaps I should be patient," mused the disappointed captain. "I've waited so many years, I guess I can wait until I get back from my trip. But wouldn't it be wonderful," he added, "if I could find her, and maybe a grandchild before I go!"

The children agreed that it would, but saw no possibility of it. Presently they bade goodbye to the captain, wishing him luck on his voyage.

As they were about to leave the hotel to go back home, they saw Miss Perkin coming toward them. The former stowaway was smiling broadly. She had on a pretty dress and looked very different from the time when she had worn boys' clothes.

"I can't tell you how happy I am to be here as an entertainer," she said to Bert and his sister. "I am earning money and getting along very nicely. I can't thank you enough, my dears."

"We're glad we could help you," spoke Nan.

"Sure!" added Bert, getting around behind his sister. He was not certain that Miss Perkin might not want to try to kiss him.

"I hope you are coming to the masquerade party tomorrow," she said.

"Yes, we're planning to," answered Nan. "Flossie and Freddie are very much excited about it."

"I know they'll have a good time," went on the entertainer who was once a stowaway. "Many of the cottage children are coming and all the hotel kiddies will be guests. There are to be prizes, good things to eat, an entertainment, and I am going to play and sing."

"Oh, I know it will be lovely," Nan said.

"Swell," agreed Bert.

Freddie was to go as a sailor and Flossie as a little fairy. Her costume was very pretty, the dress being made of white organdie. She was to carry a wand and wear a crown made of pasteboard and painted with gilt to look like gold.

Bert had made himself what he called a "pirate" suit, and Nan was to go as Little Bo Peep, the shepherdess.

"Too bad you can't take a live sheep with you!" chuckled Bert.

"As if I'd do that!" sniffed Nan.

"It would be a good idea," said her brother, laughing harder.

"Say, you're quite a good sailor!" Nan complimented her twin, when she saw him trying on his outfit.

"I hope I'll get to be," he said. "I want to win the junior cat-boat race!"

"Wouldn't it be great?" came from Nan.

At last the night of the masquerade had arrived. All was happiness and excitement for the Bobbsey twins. Their thoughts were entirely on the party they were to attend. That was what made a later happening such a complete surprise to them.

CHAPTER XXIV

A SURPRISE

THE Bobbsey twins, Freddie as a sailor, Flossie as a fairy, Nan as Bo Peep, and Bert as a pirate, all were ready, their masks in their hands. These they would put on when they reached the hotel whither they were to be driven by their father in the automobile.

"Let Dinah have a look at you before you go," suggested Mrs. Bobbsey, who was also going to the masquerade, though not in costume.

They all hurried to the kitchen.

When the colored cook saw the dressed-up twins she raised her hands above her head, laughed, and exclaimed:

"Good lan' ob massy! Yo' sho' does look sweet as sugah an' pretty as brides! Mah sakes!"

Rather pleased with themselves, the Bobbsey twins left for the party. On the way Flossie said:

"I hope I recognize Marian. She told me she'd meet me there."

"If you know how she is going to dress you can pick her out in the crowd," Bert said.

"She's going to have on an old dress her mother wore when she was a little girl. That's all I know," said Flossie.

Pirates, sailors, fairies, witches, funny people from the comic strips, Mother Goose characters, and many others were represented by the children at the Hotel Edgemere's annual masquerade party. With their masks on, the disguises were quite complete, and when Bert had donned his false face, Nan hers, and the smaller twins' features were thus hidden, it was hard for them to tell one another from the mass of other young guests.

"Say, it's a fine party, isn't it?" whispered Nan to Bert as she walked with him toward the row of chairs on one side of the ballroom.

"Yes, I guess it is," he said. "But I think I'd have more fun if I was out in my boat."

"Oh, I love a party!" murmured Nan.

Flossie and Freddie were capering about the smooth ballroom floor, laughing and squealing with other small children who were sliding on the waxed boards.

A small orchestra had been hired for the occasion. Miss Perkin was to serve as accompanist, and sing some songs. Children with their parents and friends began to arrive in a steady stream.

"Did you see Marian?" Flossie asked, sliding up to Nan, who had found a girl friend of her own age to whom she was talking.

"No, I haven't seen her yet, Flossie," was the answer. "I don't believe I'd know her if I did see her. But look around. You may be able to pick her out."

Flossie skipped away. Freddie had discovered some of his small boy friends, and Bert had struck up an acquaintance with another masked sailor about his own age. The two lads went into a corner by themselves.

To start the party, Miss Perkin played some jolly tunes and sang a number of songs. She had been very successful as a juvenile entertainer at the hotel, and Nan felt happy and proud that she had had a chance to help the stowaway secure the position. After a few minutes the teacher left the piano, spoke to the orchestra leader, and took her place in the centre of the ballroom floor.

"Now, children," she called, "get ready for the grand march. After that those of you who care to do so may dance. Later there will be a little marionette show, a Punch and Judy performance, and the real party will start with ice cream and cake."

"That's the part I want!" Freddie said out loud, making everyone laugh.

"I don't see Marian," murmured Flossie, looking about her. "She promised to meet me here."

After a few false starts the line of march was formed with Flossie and Freddie leading it, and Bert and Nan bringing up the rear among the larger children. As yet there was no sign of the little girl who had taught Flossie how to dive.

The orchestra played a lively tune. Miss Perkin looked over the line of waiting children and gave the signal.

"Forward!" she called.

The march started. Then there was a movement among the crowd at one of the doors and a little girl, attired in a quaint, old-fashioned dress, entered. Behind her was a lady, evidently her mother. The little girl was masked, but there must have been something about her that Flossie recognized, for she called out:

"Come on, Marian, get in here with me and Freddie!"

"Oh, very well, I will!" was the answer.

"I guess that's Marian, all right," said Bert, who was marching with Nan. "She looks cute."

After the young people had marched twice around the room, they were halted by a whistle.

"Children," announced Miss Perkin, "the judges have made their choices for prizes. You may take off your masks. But please march once more around the room."

As the parade started again, Nan suddenly nudged Bert's elbow.

"See Marian," she whispered. "She has taken off her mask."

"Well, what of it?" asked Bert.

"Take a good look at her, Bert!" Nan said excitedly in a low voice. "Do you notice that she resembles someone else?"

"What do you mean?" asked Bert.

"Look closely," urged his sister. "I don't want to tell you for fear I might be wrong. But doesn't she remind you of somebody?"

Bert stared at the girl diver, who was walking beside Flossie. The line of marching children was curving around the room so it was easy to get a good look at the head of the procession.

"Say, I get what you mean!" Bert exclaimed. "Marian looks like the picture the Captain showed us of his little daughter."

"Yes," said Nan, and her voice was excited.

"And doesn't she look like the picture in the charm?"

"She surely does," Bert agreed. "I wonder—you don't suppose——"

Nan was so thrilled over her idea that she stood still. Certainly Marian in the old-fashioned dress resembled very closely the likeness which Captain Van Pelt carried in his pocket—that of the little girl who had gone out of his life when he was shipwrecked.

The Bobbsey twins felt that perhaps they were on the verge of solving the strange mystery.

"I'm going to speak to Miss Perkin," said Nan, stepping out of line, and hurrying over to the teacher.

Bert followed her, and in a moment the two were speaking rapidly to the stowaway.

"Will you please tell us the last name of Marian, the girl you said was in your class?" asked Nan.

"Why, Denton."

"Oh, good!" exclaimed Nan, and Miss Perkin wondered why she had said this.

"Is her father in the insurance business?" came from Bert.

"I don't know," was the reply. "I think perhaps he is. But why do you ask?"

"Maybe something wonderful's going to happen," was Nan's comment as she dashed off with her brother toward the door.

"Shall we go to the captain's room?" asked Bert. "Oh, I hope he hasn't left yet for his trip."

"Wouldn't it be terrible if he had, and Marian should turn out to be his granddaughter!" exclaimed Nan.

The two Bobbseys were too excited to wait for the elevator. Up the stairs they went two at a time, and in a moment Bert was knocking loudly at the captain's door.

"Come in!" boomed a hearty voice.

"He's still here," breathed Nan with relief.

They quickly entered, and Bert cried out:

"Captain Van Pelt, please come with us at once."

"Why, why, what's the hurry?" the old sailor asked.

"We—we think we have a surprise for you. There's a little girl at the party downstairs we want you to see right away," explained Nan.

The Captain accompanied Bert and Nan to the gaily-decorated room. Flossie and Freddie spied the trio, and ran up to greet Captain Van Pelt. Bert then took them aside and told them that perhaps Captain Van Pelt's little granddaughter was present, but to say nothing about it just then. The little twins promised to keep the secret, but clapped their hands and were so thrilled that the old sailor could not help but notice it.

The grand march was just coming to an end, and the children were so mixed-up and confused that, though Nan wanted to find Marian, she could not at once pick out the little diver.

Suddenly, as the orchestra struck up a dance tune, Nan spied the figure of the little girl in an old-fashioned dress—that of Marian Denton. She rushed up to her, and taking her by the hand led her over to where Captain Van Pelt was talking to the other twins.

Marian looked up at the captain rather timidly. Then Nan, turning to him, said:

"This is the little girl we want you to meet. Who do you think she is?"

Flossie and Freddie were so excited they could hardly stand still, while Bert and Nan felt the same way, though they did not show it so much.

Captain Van Pelt looked long and searchingly at the figure in the old-fashioned dress. Then, his voice trembling with emotion, he cried:

"Debby! Debby! Oh, my little Deborah! Have

the Bobbsey twins found my lost daughter for me?"

Just then a lady came pushing her way through the masqueraders. Straight toward Captain Van Pelt she hurried. He was holding Marian in his arms.

"What are you doing with my little girl?" demanded the woman.

CHAPTER XXV

BERT'S RACE

CAPTAIN VAN PELT stood in the centre of the ball-room floor, holding Marian Denton in his arms. All the children had crowded around the group.

"Of course you aren't my daughter," he said sadly, after a few moments had passed. "You are too young. But you do look like the little girl I left behind when I sailed to Australia and was shipwrecked. What is your name?"

"Marian Denton," was the answer. "What's yours?"

"I am Captain Amzi Van Pelt," answered the sailor.

Upon hearing this name, the lady who had hurried over to them from a side door gave a startled cry and exclaimed:

"Then you *must* be my long lost father!"

"Oh, if that were only true," said the old man. "Are you Debby Van Pelt?"

"That was my maiden name," she answered.

"Deborah Van Pelt, but my father—and if you are my father you doubtless remember—always called me Debby."

"That's right!" cried the captain, and there were tears in his eyes. "Debby I called you and Debby I named my ship. And is this your little girl?"

"This is Marian, my daughter and your granddaughter," was the answer.

"*My very own grandfather!*" exclaimed Marian, kissing the sea captain.

"Our last name is Denton. I married a man named Denton about eight years ago," explained the lady.

"Where is he now?" asked Captain Van Pelt.

"He works in New York. Marian and I came here for the summer as my health has not been good. Oh, to think, Father, that I should find you again after all these years."

"Isn't it wonderful!" exclaimed Captain Van Pelt, while everyone about him smiled in happy surprise. "And is your mother—my wife—is she——"

"Mother died a few years after you left, and we heard nothing from you," said Mrs. Denton.

"Then it's true," murmured the captain. "Well, I couldn't expect too much happiness. It is marvelous to have found a daughter and a granddaughter. And all the credit goes to the Bobbsey twins," he added. "Do you know them?"

"I haven't met them," replied Mrs. Denton, "but I have heard Marian speak of teaching one of them to dive."

"I'm that one," said Flossie.

"And I'm Freddie. I caught a fish that had a locket in it with your picture."

As soon as the captain had introduced Bert and Nan, he pulled the charm from his pocket and showed it to his daughter to whom he told something of the little boy's adventure.

"Do you know how this got lost?" he asked.

"I can explain how it became lost," said Mrs. Denton. "You left this old charm behind, Father, when you sailed on the voyage to Australia. It had Mother's picture in it as well as my own. I always kept it. When Marian was a baby I came here for my health. I was out in a boat and the charm dropped overboard. I feared it was gone forever."

"Just what I thought about my treasure box," said the captain. "But the Bobbsey twins solved that mystery for me, too. The chest contains some trinkets I gathered in various parts of the world to give you. They are all yours, Debby and

Marian. But I should like to give each of the Bobbseys a little present from the ornaments."

"Of course, Marian and I will share our gifts with them," replied Mrs. Denton.

This was indeed a happy reunion. Marian, having found a grandfather she had heard about but had never seen, did not wish to stay at the party any longer. Neither did the captain. He wanted to get away and talk about the old, happy days.

"We'll see you Bobbsey twins again," said the old sailor, as he left with his newly-found relatives. "I want to thank you properly later."

The masquerade party was soon over. To their delight, both Flossie and Freddie each won a prize. Flossie received a painting set and her twin a kite. Nan and Bert were happy in musing about how they had helped Captain Van Pelt solve the mystery.

"And to think," said the captain a few days later, when he called at Buttonball Cottage with his daughter and Marian, "that I named my schooner *Debby D,* and that the 'D' I happened to pick out should be the initial of my daughter's married name. Oh, it's all very strange!"

"Did you find it was really your daughter who had signed the visitors' book at Old Church?"

"Yes, it was," answered the sailor. "A good many years before she was married she visited the place with her mother."

Mr. and Mrs. Bobbsey rejoiced with the captain in his happiness. He explained that he had been able to postpone his trip to South America for a week. He declared they must all come for a visit to his schooner. This they did. The captain made a regular party of it, with ice cream, cake, and other good things to eat.

Mr. Green, the parrot, talked his loudest, much to the delight of Marian and her mother. Pegleg Baldwin showed them not only the green lion tattooed on his chest but a red tiger on one shoulder, too.

"I'm going to put one like that on me!" declared Freddie. "Flossie won a new set of paints and I'm thinking about making pictures on my chest."

"Not while you live at home!" said his father, laughing.

It was indeed a happy time for all. When Bert happened to mention that in a few days the hotel regatta was to be held and that he was going to enter the *Fairy* in the junior division, Captain Van Pelt said:

"Then I must give you a few more lessons. I

want to see you win that race, Bert. You and the other twins helped me a lot and I want to help you."

Under the expert advice of the sailor, Bert learned a few new points about sailing that stood him in good stead. On the day of the race the captain and his daughter, with Marian, the three Bobbsey twins, and their father and mother, joined the crowd on the bay shore to watch the junior race.

Bert's entry, the *Fairy,* and several other small cat boats crossed the line quite evenly at the crack of the starting pistol. Then the race really began.

It was a triangular course. The contestants were to start from a point near the public dock, sail out around one flag on a wooden float, then around another flag, and finally back to the starting place.

The wind was fresh and the boats heeled sharply.

"Oh, Bert will tip over!" cried Flossie.

"Well, he can swim," said Freddie.

Bert, however, did not upset, though one boat did. But the small skipper was quickly rescued. The others sailed on. Bert was ahead at the turn of the first flag, but lost a little going toward the second. When he rounded that one, two other boats were ahead of him.

"Oh, he isn't going to win!" said Nan.

"Just you wait!" cried Captain Van Pelt. "I've taught Bert a trick or two. He knows how to sail close to the wind and that's what he has to do now."

As Bert's friends watched, he slowly drew up on even terms with the two leaders after rounding the second flag. In coming along the last leg of the triangular course, Bert handled his craft so expertly that he got a good position and crossed the finish line a winner by three lengths when the final pistol shot of the judges rang out.

So Bert won the small silver cup which was the prize for skippers under the age of twelve sailing their own boats.

"I'm quite proud of you, my boy!" said his father when Bert came ashore.

"Oh, what a lovely summer this has been!" said Nan, when they were on their way back to the cottage.

"Yes, it was great," Bert agreed, "even when we were chased by the bear."

"That was fun, after it was all over!" laughed Nan.

Captain Van Pelt stayed with his daughter and granddaughter, and met Mr. Denton a few days later. Then he got ready to sail for South America, a happier man than he had been for many, many years. Before leaving, the captain gave each of the Bobbsey twins a souvenir from his treasure box.

This made them very happy and kept them thinking about the kindly old man for a long while—until, in fact, another trip came to them. It is called "The Bobbsey Twins on a Ranch."

During the remainder of this vacation the Bobbsey twins had good times and lots of fun at Storm Haven. They all agreed, however, that the happiest time of all was when they solved the mystery.

THE END